THE PHANTOM STRIKES

The desert terrain was once haunted by the Phantom — a blanched man on a pale-grey horse, who struck in the night and killed without mercy. Wild Bill Hickok shot the legend down once — and twenty years later, when the Phantom's son took up the torch, he did so again . . . With both culprits dead, Hickok and his compadres are satisfied they have laid the ghost to rest. But when a mortally wounded man gasps that the spirit has returned, they must take up arms once more — against the Phantom's second son . . .

Books by Walt Keene
in the Linford Western Library:

THE BRAND-BURNERS
GUN FURY
THE PHANTOM RIDER

WALT KEENE

THE PHANTOM STRIKES

Complete and Unabridged

LINFORD
Leicester

First published in Great Britain in 2013 by
Robert Hale Limited
London

First Linford Edition
published 2015
by arrangement with
Robert Hale Limited
London

A catalogue record for this book is available
from the British Library.

ISBN 978–1–4448–2573–2

Published by
F. A. Thorpe (Publishing)
Anstey, Leicestershire

Set by Words & Graphics Ltd.
Anstey, Leicestershire
Printed and bound in Great Britain by
T. J. International Ltd., Padstow, Cornwall

This book is printed on acid-free paper

Dedicated to Clint Eastwood

Prologue

The sky was blue. The only clouds were memories. The arid desert landscape sizzled like bacon frying in a skillet beneath the sun's unrelenting rays and anything alive also fried. There was no mercy in this place; people lived beneath the unyielding sun because they had nowhere else to go. For the settlers who had reached the barren wastelands decades earlier and had chosen to put down roots this was better than the places where they had originated. Although it resembled something crafted by the Devil himself, the settlers knew that true Hell was far behind them back in the overcrowded East. For poverty and despair had beset these souls; now, those conditions were no more than a memory.

Although the desert region was harsh people had survived and prospered in a way that necessity can drive those with faith to do.

Towns had managed to spring up throughout the once-empty land and although many had soon been abandoned a few had stubbornly flourished. For men are not like beasts and where no water can be seen they tend to dig. Countless wells had been dug in the baking-hot sand and some had found something far more precious than gold. They had located water, which was the key to survival.

Yet water could not solve all their problems. They had to endeavour in their personal trades to create something that every one of them knew the desert could snatch from them at any time.

The desert could never truly be tamed, only suppressed. Yet for all its dangers and natural perils there was another more horrific thing to fear. It was something which had been spawned in ancient myth and had somehow grown like a cancer into the realms of fact.

The treacherous desert had a rival. A living monster in human form which had proved to be far more lethal than anything nature had yet to create.

Shadows crossed the blistering-hot sand as a pair of black vultures floated aloft on thermals, searching for their next meal. The desert always provided the creatures that lived off the less fortunate with plenty of easy pickings. Death came easily in the land that stretched from horizon to horizon, for it took no prisoners. Bleached bones littered the sand. The foolhardy usually paid the ultimate price for underestimating its power over mere mortals, but there was another far more merciless danger lurking in the arid landscape.

For this was the land of the deadly horseman known as the Phantom. A myth, a legend who had become a reality.

For decades stories of the albino rider who killed every man, woman and child who had the misfortune to get into his gun sights filled the souls of those who lived in and around the desert. Then the creature who looked as though every drop of blood had been drained from his face and body suddenly came to life.

Twenty years previously a maniac who fitted perfectly the description of the horrific legend had emerged from the desert and senselessly killed everyone who got in his way. After what had seemed like a lifetime to those who lived in fear of the Phantom striking at them and their loved ones, he simply vanished again.

The people from Cactus Flats to Rio Hondo had thought their prayers had been answered. A miracle had happened and they had been saved.

It made no sense to anyone, but the insane Phantom had disappeared as suddenly as he had emerged. The brutal slaughter had ceased and then, over the next two decades, had once again become nothing more than a tall tale. Soon the stories would be regarded as nothing more than the fertile imaginings of the old-timers.

Then it happened again.

It seemed impossible, but the lethal killer who had waged war on the innocent people of the region twenty years earlier had come back to life once more.

Those who had set eyes upon the original monster swore that the new Phantom was the same man. Everything about him was identical, yet how could a man not age a single day in more than twenty years? A living man would have grown older but a real monster might not.

A new fear swept through the land of myths. Had everyone been wrong all those years ago? Had the brutal slayer actually been a real monster after all? Something that was not human, but part of the deadly desert itself?

Had Satan actually allowed one of his monstrous underlings to set foot upon the land of the living?

The rider had exactly matched the description of the original Phantom when he appeared in the same region once again. Just as before, he killed without mercy and for no better reason than that he simply was able to do so.

He had the same features, which were devoid of pigment. The same long white hair and beard, which seemed to have been fashioned in the nightmares of all who set eyes upon him.

He wore the same small black-glass spectacles protecting his eyes. Just as before, this creature rode a pale-grey mount and only struck during the hours of darkness. When the sun rose the Phantom was gone and would not reappear until night fell once again.

Yet this abominable mass murderer was no mythical being, as so many had grown to believe and fear. He was of flesh and blood like all of his victims.

Unknown to most who tasted his wrath, the new Phantom was in reality an escaped lunatic. He was also the son of the original man monster who had christened himself the Phantom after the ancient legend.

Twenty years earlier Axil Gunn had gone steadily insane in the harsh landscape in which he had grown up. For an albino the desert was the worst climate he could ever have had the misfortune to be raised in. It had crippled an already fragile mind. He had been married to a Cree woman and fathered two sons. Both, like their father, were albinos.

As his mind had melted and his inner torment had grown Axil Gunn learned of the legend of the Phantom. Knowing that he fitted the description of the Phantom perfectly, he had become that creature and had set out on a path of total bloody destruction.

His rampage had instilled trepidation into the people who lived in the hot, unforgiving terrain. The Phantom's atrocities went unchecked until one man stopped him permanently after a gun fight that lasted for hours.

Suddenly the Phantom had vanished into the heat haze of myths and the Almighty had been praised for the people's salvation. The true hero had never mentioned his part in stopping the mayhem until twenty years had passed and a new identical Phantom emerged.

Only when the avenging son of Axil Gunn escaped from an asylum in Badwater and headed south towards the place where his father had once roamed did the legendary James Butler Hickok announce to his two friends Tom Dix and Dan Shaw that, contrary to what folks were saying about the Phantom, the truth was it could not be the same man. The reason the new albino horseman had not aged in over twenty years was because he was not the same man.

Hickok explained to his pals that he had killed the original Phantom in one of his bloodiest encounters. Then he recalled that Axil Gunn had two albino sons. Two souls who, like Gunn himself, did not have an ounce of colour in their entire bodies.

The new Phantom had to be one of those sons. If he was correct, Hickok told his friends, he knew where Gunn and his family had lived, up high in the mesas that loomed over the desert.

In a valiant attempt to stop the slaughter from continuing, Hickok, Dix and Shaw set out for the Phantom's stronghold.

Once more Wild Bill vowed that he would stop the new Phantom just as he had stopped the original. Few men ever had cause to kill the same monster twice and Hickok did not relish the job he had chosen for himself, for unlike the legendary Phantom, he was twenty years older and past his prime.

The three veteran riders rode out to the distant mesas knowing full well that the Phantom was far younger than anyone dreamed and would be a hard man to stop, possibly even harder to stop than his father had been.

The battle had been a long-drawn-out affair in the same mountainous crags where the original showdown had taken place. The only difference was that this time the famed Hickok was not alone. Both Dan Shaw and Tom

Dix had vainly tried to help but they simply could not pin down the albino gunman. The high rocks were riddled with cave tunnels and no sooner had the three trained their weapons on their target than he disappeared in one of the caves. Then as if by some magical trick he reappeared from another of the cave openings.

Hickok's first encounter with the creature who claimed to be the mythical Phantom had been a battle but this soon became a war.

A war of attrition which only the fittest would survive.

Then when it looked as though Axil Gunn's equally insane son was about to kill both Dix and Shaw the legendary Wild Bill Hickok displayed the speed of cross-draw gunplay for which he was famed.

For the second time, James Butler Hickok had killed the Phantom and stopped further senseless slayings. Once again Hickok had survived as only legends can survive, and he and his best friends rode away from their triumphant victory knowing that none of them would ever mention what they had done.

Legends never die easily.

What none of the three riders was aware of was that the albino gunman they had fought and killed up in the high mesas was not the escaped lunatic who had slaughtered his way south from the Badwater asylum.

They had killed his identical brother.

Wounded, Enio Gunn had watched Hickok, Dix and Shaw ride away as he stood beside his mother on the high cliff top beside the dead albino. The old Cree woman took her son by his arm and led him into one of the caves.

She would tend his wounds and poison his mind, as she had done all his life. When Gunn was healed the Phantom would strike again. This time it would be with even more venomous revenge in his heartless soul.

James Butler Hickok thought it was over.

Yet legends never die easily.

1

The ox-drawn covered wagon meandered through the desert as the last throes of night gave way to the coming of a new day. The canvas canopy concealed its deadly cargo from prying eyes as the old Cree woman steered the weathered vehicle on towards another secret place, where they would seek refuge. The grey horse tethered to the wooden tailgate was saddled and ready to obey its master's every command. There was an urgency in the old woman as she guided the ox to the place of which only she and her son knew. It was one of countless places in the desert that, she knew, would allow her demented offspring to rest during the hours of daylight. For Enio Gunn, like his late brother and father before him, was a man without pigment.

An albino. One who could never

allow the torturous rays of the desert sun to rest for even a few moments upon his white, sensitive flesh.

One by one the stars faded into the slowly increasing light that spread across the heavens. But sunrise was still a long way off. There was still plenty of time for them to reach their destination. Then in the distance a dust cloud rose behind an approaching stagecoach as it navigated between the jagged mesas and journeyed on towards its next port of call, Rio Hondo. It caught the old woman's attention. As always the Cree woman was the flame that ignited her men's fuses.

She stopped the wagon, leaned back and spoke to her resting son in the darkness of the vehicle's interior. 'Enio, my son. We have fresh prey.'

Unaware of what they were heading towards the driver and his shotgun guard sat aloft on the high, well-sprung board and drove their fresh team towards the rocky mesas. They had only just left the way station at Apache

Springs and were refreshed. They had only one fare-paying passenger. Chuck Franks had been driving for nearly two days without sleep but that was nothing new to the sturdy, well-built man.

When he had reached Rio Hondo he would be able to sleep for days if he chose. Yet men cut from Franks's kind of cloth seldom slept. They had far better things to do with their time away from their distant wives. Rio Hondo did not have much, but it had a lot of friendly women and enough whiskey to drown in.

Franks had always enjoyed both.

He brought his whip down across the backs of his six-horse team and encouraged them to maintain their pace. He could taste the whiskey and smell the perfume of what he knew lay thirty miles ahead of them.

Then, as the stagecoach raced up a steep incline and crossed over the hunchback of a ridge, something caught Franks's eye about a mile ahead.

'Do ya see that, Buck?' the driver

yelled out over the sound of the pounding hoofs beneath their high vantage point.

The alert guard squinted hard and stared at what his partner was looking at. Holden gazed ahead into the strange light. A light only found during the twilight period between night and day.

'I see something sure enough,' Holden said.

'What the hell is it, Buck?' Franks shouted out again as he kept thrashing the hefty reins across the backs of the galloping team.

'I ain't sure.' The guard reached down into the box and pulled up his scattergun from its hiding-place beside the stagecoach strongbox. He rested the twin-barrelled shotgun across his knees and continued to stare ahead. 'Whatever it is we're headed straight at it.'

Franks kept forging on. 'Is it on the road?'

'I ain't sure,' the guard answered nervously. 'I reckon ya better haul rein in case it is, Chuck. We don't want to wreck the stage out here.'

'Right.' The anxious driver pressed his boot on the long brake pole and slowly pushed it down. The stagecoach slowed but did not stop. Franks kept his team moving as he strained his eyes in an attempt to identify the object. The six horses cantered towards the strange sight, now less than a few hundred yards away. 'Can ya make out what in tarnation it is now? Is it a barricade?'

Buck Holden curled a finger around the two triggers of the shotgun. He raised the heavy weapon and aimed its barrels at the apparition. Suddenly realization engulfed him.

'Don't stop, Chuck. Whatever ya do, don't stop,' Holden urged as panic swept over him. 'Whatever that is, it sure ain't no barricade.'

'Damn it all!' the driver snarled. 'Make up ya mind. I'll have to stop if the road's blocked, Buck. I can't risk steering this thing on to the sand. We'll turn over for certain.'

Buck Holden stood in the box and

raised the scattergun up to his shoulder. 'I'm telling ya. Don't stop.'

Franks glanced up at the guard. 'Why not?'

The guard swallowed hard. 'Because I can see it clear now.'

'What in tarnation is it?' the driver's voice screamed out. 'What can ya see? What? What?'

'A man on horseback,' Holden replied. 'But it ain't like no man I ever done set eyes on before, Chuck. Whip ya team. Whip 'em hard. Ride through the thing.'

Franks was confused. His eyes darted between his guard and the object ahead of them. Then to his horror he too saw it as clearly as his partner. His eyes widened in shock at what they were looking upon. The colourless horseman draped in a bleached long coat sat like a statue atop the lean grey stallion, watching the stagecoach from the very middle of the dusty road. The black circular-lensed spectacles he wore glinted in the changing light.

'Holy smoke, Buck!' Franks yelled out at the top of his lungs. 'What is he? I never seen any man look like him before.'

'The Phantom,' the guard gasped in horror.

'Can't be,' the driver shouted as he kept his team approaching. 'Can it?'

'Whip them horses, Chuck,' Buck pleaded as he kept staring along the length of his twin barrels. 'Whoever he is, he sure don't look friendly, and he sure looks like the stories I've heard of the Phantom.'

Franks slapped his long leathers down hard on the backs of the six horses before them. 'If ya right we're dead men. That critter kills everything he sets eyes on.'

The words could not have been more true.

Within seconds the Phantom tapped his spurs and made his mount walk back a few strides as he drew a pair of deadly .45s from his holsters and cocked their hammers. Then, as his

19

white hands raised the weapons, he swung his horse to face the coach.

Enio Gunn emotionlessly aimed the Colts straight at the approaching men who were seated high on the stagecoach's running-board. They had nowhere to hide. There was a cold, calculated inevitability in the way Gunn treated all of his potential victims. Not one drop of precious mercy had ever flowed through his emaciated body.

Everyone was his enemy.

Everyone had to pay the ultimate price.

That had been driven into his very soul by the old Cree woman throughout his entire life. Like so many other mindless creatures who become the puppets of the insane, Gunn believed every poisonous word she uttered.

Enio Gunn was her instrument of savage revenge. He, like his brother and father before him, did as he was told. He killed their enemies without question with no more compunction than someone stepping on an ant.

Another heartbeat later and both his guns spewed out two flashes of deafening venom.

Shafts of fiery lead sped through the plumes of gunsmoke and headed for their targets. Buck Holden felt the bullet punch him backwards. His shotgun blasted heavenwards as he crashed against the metal luggage rail. His fingers fumbled in his coat pocket for two fresh cartridges as another of the Phantom's bullets hit him.

Franks watched helplessly as his friend tumbled from the running-board and disappeared into the cloud of hoof dust. The frantic driver dragged his trusty bullwhip from beside him and lashed its fourteen-foot length down across the backs of his team. Instantly the horses reacted and bolted ahead at even greater speed.

The Phantom raised his thin arms and cocked the hammers of his smoking weapons again, just as the stagecoach thundered past the unearthly-looking horseman. *I'm still alive*, he thought, as he kept screaming down at the team. *Still alive and still in one piece.*

Then Franks heard another volley of gunfire from behind him. The sound of the passenger inside the coach screaming as bullets ripped through the wooden sides of the vehicle and hit him filled the driver's ears. Franks leaned forward, then he too screamed out in agony.

It felt as though a sabre had been thrust through him.

Franks had watched in horror as his chest exploded outwards and a bullet passed through his torso. A mass of gore had sprayed over the horses beneath him as they charged on. He leaned back and knew that finally his luck had run out. One of the Phantom's bullets had carved a route into his back and out of his chest.

Somehow he managed to defy his unimaginable pain and injury and keep whipping his team of horses.

'Faster. Faster,' Franks yelled out.

The sound of gunfire continued

echoing around the desert until the stagecoach was out of the Phantom's lethal range. Yet Franks was unable to stop whipping his horses. Unable to stop driving them on towards their distant destination at breakneck speed.

The instinct to survive now controlled the critically wounded driver. There was no thought behind his actions any longer. Now Chuck Franks was merely a creature desperate to flee death itself, unaware that it was already riding beside him on the high running-board.

Then the sun rose, but Franks did not notice its blinding light as it spread like a wildfire across the arid landscape that surrounded the stagecoach. He kept on driving across the dry desert as he had done hundreds of times before.

This time was different though. Franks was all but dead, but sometimes men refuse to die.

Sometimes they are too frightened to die.

2

It was said that there was no sweeter water anywhere within a hundred square miles than that which could be found in the remote desert town of Rio Hondo. The rambling settlement only existed because a decade earlier twenty deep wells had been dug in its white sand. Somewhere deep in the otherwise arid landscape there was a lake of precious water and the stubborn town's elders had found it. That act of blind faith had put the town on the stagecoach route and the Overland Stagecoach company had been quick to use its obvious benefits. Virtually overnight Rio Hondo became a vital link which allowed the far-flung desert settlements to become accessible to one another after years of separation.

Yet times were still hard for those who chose to remain on the otherwise barren terrain. Apart from the regular stagecoaches that visited daily there was little other enterprise, but the people of Rio Hondo were tough and resilient and never quit or despaired. They had a faith common in the wildest parts of the West.

Nothing had ever broken their spirits.

Nothing ever left them downhearted for long. There was always another new day just beyond the last whispers of night.

A better day than any that had gone before.

The stark truth though was that this was still a cruel land and only those who had faith had ever managed to survive its perilous wrath intact. Bodies might have been broken on occasion but never the determined spirits of the men and women who dared nature with every new dawn.

Yet even the toughest of the people who resided in Rio Hondo were still licking their wounds from the savage attacks that had occurred only forty days before. They, like those who lived in every other settlement in the remote desert, had tasted the bullets of the Phantom. They were still licking their wounds and fearful that the ghostlike creature would return one dark night.

It had only been five weeks since the two veteran riders Tom Dix and Dan Shaw had thought they had witnessed the death of the albino maniac known as the Phantom. They had seen how their old friend Wild Bill Hickok had fearlessly outdrawn the unholy Axil Gunn, and they imagined, as had Hickok himself, that that had to be the end of the sickening story.

The fearless trio had left Gunn dead up on the high plateau, but they were unaware that they had killed the wrong Gunn. Hickok's bullets had destroyed the Phantom's brother.

Unknown to the three intrepid avengers it had been Enio Gunn who had slaughtered his way south from the insane asylum back to his mother and identical sibling. Although he had also tasted the lead of Hickok and his two comrades, Enio Gunn was far from dead.

After the brutal battle the famed ex-lawman, war hero and gambler James Butler Hickok had waved fare-well to Dix and Shaw. Hickok had gone on his way seeking whiskey, women and new opponents to play poker with whilst his two old friends had remained in the area picking up occasional work wherever they could find it.

Unlike Hickok their pockets were not filled with the winnings from gambling. Dix and Shaw needed money in order to buy provisions so that they could continue the search for a place where they might find peace.

As with most strangers to the long strip of sand and high mesas, they desired little more than to escape the merciless land in which they had found them-selves trapped. They desired a less torturous climate, but that required money.

It mattered little how brave a soul was.

Even the bravest of men needed to eat and drink and that had started to prove a difficult habit to maintain in a place where jobs were as scarce as hen's teeth.

Dan Shaw was a retired lawman and entitled to a pension but out here in the desert there was no way he could get his hands on a penny of it. The closest thing to a bank was fifty miles away in Cactus Flats.

His pal Tom Dix had once been a famed gun fighter. He had hired his gun skills out to anyone who had the high price he had demanded, but all that had changed a long time before. Now that life was little more than a distant and sickening memory, which he had vainly tried to forget. Dix was still fast with his .45s but age had taken the fire from his belly. He no longer hired his once unrivalled abilities out to the men who wanted him to destroy their enemies.

Since the battle up in the high mesas Dix had not even touched his guns.

Now it was becoming obvious to both the seasoned riders that they would have to find jobs soon if they were to eat again.

Rio Hondo was just getting itself prepared for the coming of nightfall as Dix and Dan steered their horses into the small town. The two horsemen watched as men lit the coal tar lanterns along the main thoroughfare as the sky above them turned scarlet. Neither had spoken for more than an hour since they had returned from yet another fruitless ride to and from a ranch situated in the hottest part of the desert. It seemed that ranchers liked their wranglers young and naïve and it had been a long time since Dix and Dan had been either.

They had not eaten anything for more than two days and their innards were growling like a pair of old pumas. The town was quiet. Too quiet.

It seemed strange to both riders how few people remained on its streets even though the sun had not set. Perhaps the recent events across the desert had scared every living creature within its boundaries. The coming of nightfall had meant the Phantom might strike until only a short while before. Even though the slaughtering had stopped, some folks took a long time to get over such things.

Dix reined in first. The noise from the solitary saloon filled both men's ears, but they silently knew they could not afford even a short beer, let alone anything more substantial. Then the wonderful aroma of cooking filled their nostrils as it drifted from the town's two cafés. It lingered on the late-afternoon air and tormented both the veteran riders.

Their guts began to grumble even more loudly.

The fading rays of the setting sun seemed to catch every pane of glass in the street's windows and doors. The riders turned their horses towards a trough and hitching rail near a shuttered hardware store.

The dazzling display did not impress either of the men who sat astride their lathered-up mounts. All they could think about was the fact that they were hungry. Really hungry.

'Got any ideas, Dixie?' Dan asked. He eased himself off his horse and rested his back against a hitching rail, his gloved fingers toying with his long leathers.

Dix sighed, then dismounted. He exhaled loudly and patted his flat stomach as if trying to get it to quieten.

A wry smile crossed his unshaven face. 'Ever wondered what horse tastes like, Dan?'

Both men laughed.

Dan Shaw looked at their horses. 'Yep. The more I look at these pitiful critters the more I reckon it might be worth trying to find out.'

'We sure need a job,' Dix said.

'Don't fret none. We'll get us a job.' Dan nodded. 'There must be something we can do around here that'll pay us enough to buy us some vittles.'

Dix grinned. 'Damned if I can think of anything. They ain't even got a sheriff here, so hiring on as deputies ain't on the cards.'

Suddenly the unmistakable sound of a racing stagecoach echoed around the pair of hungry drifters. Every wall of every building resounded with the pounding of hoofs and a cracking whip. Dan Shaw straightened up and looked at his partner. 'Hear that, Dixie?'

Dix gave a knowing nod. He knew all too well what was making the sound. He grabbed the mane of his tall mount and turned the animal. 'Sounds like a runaway stage to me, Dan.'

'It sure does.'

Dix tightened the drawstring of his hat under his chin and stepped away from his pal. 'I got me a gut feeling that some poor critter's in trouble. Big trouble.'

Both men stepped ahead of their horses and stared curiously along the street in the direction of the frantic sound that echoed off the wooden structures.

Then they saw it.

The wide eyes of the six-horse team mirrored those of the driver as he drove the vehicle straight into the dying rays of the setting sun. A devilish red glow illuminated the fast-moving vehicle as it rocked unsteadily behind the pounding hoofs of its racing team.

'Is that driver loco?' Dan asked. He moved away from his exhausted animal. 'He'll turn that coach over if he keeps cracking that whip over them horses like that. He'll break his neck or worse. What's wrong with him?'

Dix did not answer. This was no time for words. This was a time for action. He swung himself back up on to his high saddle, hauled the horse round and spurred. Dust kicked up as the old gunfighter defied his years and fearlessly galloped towards the approaching stagecoach.

With each stride of his horse Dix could see the driver more clearly in the strange light as the swaying stagecoach drew closer. Dix squinted, then saw the dark stain in the middle of the driver's shirt. The dying rays of crimson light which bathed the horses, the conveyance and the driver could not hide the bullet hole in the man's chest from Tom Dix's knowing eyes.

The seasoned horseman steered his mount directly at the oncoming stagecoach. He saw the desperate driver crack his whip high above his head. It was if the driver was in a trance and no longer knew what he was doing. Every movement was now nothing more than well-practised habit.

Dix drove his mount on. Then at the very last moment he yanked his horse to one side as the team of horses swept past him. He spurred in pursuit. He leaned across the neck of his galloping mount and spurred again. The rider reached the large rear wheel of the stage, then he cracked his reins across the rump of his mount. The tall stallion found more pace and kept on charging until Dix was right below the driver's box. It was like an ancient chariot race

34

as the horseman kept level with the speeding vehicle.

He hurriedly drew his right boot from his stirrup and brought it up until it was on top of his saddle. Dix forced his entire body upward, then leapt. His gloved hands grabbed hold of the edge of the driver's box. The stagecoach showed no sign of slowing down as it thundered along the narrow street, and Dix hauled his lean body up until he was on the long driver's board.

Dix tore the reins from the man's grip and pulled back as his right boot forced the brake pole forward. The sound of the brakes screeching echoed around the small town. A cloud of dust billowed up from the wheels as they ceased turning.

The long vehicle came to a sudden halt.

Before Dix could loop the heavy leathers around the pole to secure it the driver slumped over on to the flat, well-sprung board beside him. People suddenly filled the darkening street from every doorway, but Dix did not notice any of them as he leaned over the stricken driver.

Dix stood in the box and leaned close to the wounded man. He patted his cheek. The unblinking man mumbled as though he were trying to describe a nightmare. None of his words made any sense to the gunfighter.

'What ya trying to say, buddy?' Dix vainly asked. The man coughed and blood trailed from the corner of his mouth. His hands shook feebly.

Dix carefully eased the driver on to his side. More blood trickled from his open mouth. The wounded man stared into Dix's face like a child seeking reassurance. Dix glanced down at the driver's shirt. His jaw dropped at the horrific sight that greeted his eyes.

The shirt was torn apart both front and back. A bullet had gone clean through the driver. The hole in his chest was larger than the one in his back. Dix knew that meant only one thing.

'You were back-shot,' Dix muttered.

Somehow the determined driver had not died even after having his torso blown apart. Dix marvelled at the willpower it must have required for him to keep the stagecoach going after he had been shot in the back.

'Who did this, friend?' Dix whispered, as the street started to fill with curious townspeople who had heard the frantic approach of the stagecoach. 'Who shot you? Tell me who did this.'

The man's bloody gloved hand gripped Dix's shirtsleeve and squeezed hard. He turned his head and looked into the weathered old face.

'The Phantom,' he stammered.

'What?' The veteran gunfighter could not believe his ears.

'The Phantom,' the driver repeated. 'He's come back from the dead again.'

Stunned, Tom Dix straightened up and watched the driver as he finally closed his eyes. The fingers released their grip from Dix's sleeve and his arm fell limply away.

People started to climb up the side of

the stagecoach as Dix stepped up on to its roof and walked across it until he reached its end. Dix eased himself down and used the large rear wheel to ease his descent to the ground.

Dan rushed up to his bewildered friend.

'You OK, Dixie?' Dan asked. 'What's wrong?'

Dix glanced at his friend. 'He said the Phantom shot him, Dan. That ain't possible, is it?'

Dan patted his pal on the back. 'It sure ain't. We know that for sure. The Phantom's dead. We saw Wild Bill kill the bastard weeks back. There ain't no way that stagecoach driver could have been shot by the Phantom, Dixie. Maybe ya heard him wrong.'

'I know what he said, Dan.' Tom Dix walked over to his horse, which had come to a stop in the middle of the street. He grabbed its reins, then paused.

'But it's impossible,' Dan protested.

'Listen up. He said the Phantom has

come back from the dead again,' Dix told him. 'Chew on that.'

Dan Shaw rubbed his neck. 'But he's dead.'

'He was dead before, Dan.' Dix walked past his pal, leading his horse behind him. 'Maybe all those stories about him not being like other folks are true. Maybe he ain't a man like you and me. We both know James Butler killed him. Not once but twice. Now he seems to have come back from the dead for a third time. Whatever that white-skinned varmint critter is, he sure don't die easy.'

Dan followed his confused friend along the street. 'Bill killed two different *hombres*, Dixie. The father twenty years back and then the son. They're two different bastards.'

Tom Dix stopped abruptly and looked over one broad shoulder. 'Hold on a minute, pard. There was another son according to James Butler. Remember?'

'Holy smoke. That's right,' Dan

gasped. 'There must have been another of them Gunn boys up in them caves. That's why he could move so fast and kept getting the drop on us. We were fighting two critters and didn't know it. Wild Bill killed one but we must have left the other one up there in one of them caves. Damn it all. We left another loco Phantom alive.'

Dix sighed. 'And now he's back doing what the Phantom always does. Killing folks.'

A stout man emerged from the crowd and began to gesture to them. Dix and Dan watched as the man walked up to them and then stopped. He looked the pair up and down.

'My name's Carter Drew,' the man said, looking at Dix. 'I liked the way you handled yourself.'

'Howdy, Mr Drew.' Dix touched his hat brim. 'This is my pard, Dan. He used to be a lawman.'

'Can we do something for you?' Dan added.

'You sure can. I run the Overland

Stagecoach Rio Hondo depot,' Drew said in a low, cold tone. 'I've got two job vacancies if you boys are interested. I've a schedule to keep. This coach has to be driven back to Cactus Flats via the way station at Apache Springs in the morning. Are you interested?'

'If the pay's right we are.' Dan nodded.

'I'll pay top dollar and a bonus if you boys get that coach back to Cactus Flats without getting any of the passengers shot up.' Drew stared at both men.

Dan looked back at the lifeless body of the stagecoach driver, which was being carefully handed down from his high perch and carried away. He then looked at Drew.

'Two job vacancies? I count only one.'

'I said two vacancies and that's what I meant.' Carter Drew raised his eyebrows. 'There was a guard on that stage with Chuck. I have an inkling he didn't do a whole lot better than Chuck or their passenger did. Now, are you interested?'

Both men nodded and without any hesitation spoke at the same time.

'Yep,' they said.

3

Another night took hold across the desert. The heat which had tormented the hours of daylight suddenly gave way to a bone-chilling frost. Countless stars and a crescent moon cast their eerie light down across the vast expanse of sand that went from horizon to horizon. The high mesas looked like nightmarish monsters as they loomed over the sparkling terrain. It grew colder with every passing moment. There were a thousand caves set in the walls of the moonlit rocks, but few people had ever set foot in any of them.

Only those who sought the sanctuary of the dark recesses carved out over a million years by nature had ever ventured into their black bellies.

The old Cree woman and her hideous remaining son were two of the few people who had. It paid to be cautious even when you were a loathsome slaughterer of innocents. Although the old woman had never actually killed anyone herself, she had fuelled the hatred in her menfolk which had destroyed so many poor souls. There was an old saying that hatred is infectious and the Cree woman had proved it to be correct.

Some waged war for their chosen gods. Some considered the words of their prophets to be so precious and holy that they had to obey them without question. There were others who were just so simple-minded that they obeyed their betters without ever questioning them. The Gunn menfolk had all been equally simple and that, mixed with an inherited streak of insanity, had made them lethal killers.

Whatever injustice had originally poisoned the mind of the old Cree woman into wanting her men to kill every living person they encountered would never be known. It had burned itself like a branding-iron into the deepest, darkest corners of her twisted brain. Now every evil thought fermented in the cesspit of demons that was all that remained of her mind.

For decades she had moved unseen around the desert with her menfolk until there was only one left. She knew every cave and every black shadow.

Although not an albino herself the old woman had grown used to living as they were forced to live. She lived in the shadows. She existed only during the hours of darkness, as her men did.

The covered wagon stood where they had left it the previous night at the foot of the steep rocky mountainside whilst the big ox ate the food its demented masters had set down for it. The huge beast chewed on its hay and remained attached to its traces. Unlike the albino cargo it had hauled to this place, it had no desire to harm anyone or anything. The grey stallion was still tied to the wagon's tailgate as it too ate its meagre daily ration.

Darkness had come once again. With

it a fully rested murderer was about to set out on another night of mindless slaughter. His mother had told him that the desert belonged to them and every man, woman and child who invaded their sacred land had to pay the ultimate price.

Enio Gunn had no thoughts of his own in his rancid mind. He had ceased being able to think for himself long ago. Now his every thought belonged not to himself, but to the female who had planted the seeds of hatred in him.

He was nothing more than a killing machine. Just like his father before him, he carried out his mother's commands. He killed because that was what he did. He had actually become the Phantom, both in body and soul.

Gunn had slept for more than twenty-four hours since he had attacked the stagecoach. Now he was refreshed and desired to continue his atrocities. A new night offered new victims and the chance that he might find his most sought-after prey. Hickok had killed his father and his brother and had even wounded him. To Gunn that was more than enough reasons for him to want revenge. He would not rest until he had killed the famed Wild Bill Hickok.

The Phantom would slay everyone who got in his way until Hickok returned once again to the desert. Gunn was certain of it. Hickok had claimed he had finished the mythical creature and would not wish to look as though he had lied. The albino murderer knew the legendary Wild Bill's pride and vanity would never allow another Phantom to exist.

The ghostlike creature checked his guns. Gunn was ready once again to sprinkle the tempting crumbs he knew would lure the famed Hickok into his trap. When it became known that the Phantom was once more terrorizing the desert region Hickok would be unable to resist returning to finish a job he had already considered done. Although totally insane the last of the Gunn men-folk was cunning enough to know men like Hickok could be drawn to bait as easily as anyone else. When you were hunting one of the best scouts in the West you had to ensure that he did not suspect the truth. Hickok had to think he was the hunter when in fact he was the hunted.

He was Enio Gunn's prey.

At long last the son of Axil Gunn would get his revenge, not just for his father and brother but for the fact that it had been Hickok himself who had ensured his being locked up in an asylum for years.

A place in which Gunn would still have been rotting if not for the fact that he had managed to slaughter his way to freedom.

The pale-skinned man walked from one of the cave entrances known only to his mother and himself high on the mountainside and made his silent way down to where his horse nervously waited. Soon the grey stallion would again feel the razor-sharp spurs of its merciless master.

Gunn had recovered well from the bullet wounds he had suffered when he and his brother had taken on Hickok and his two friends. His mother had used her medicine chest of herbs and lotions and brought the last of her menfolk back to full health. Her strange tonic, made by fermenting various desert plants, helped keep any hope of sanity from returning to her son. His mind was hers to control when he was intoxicated by the dangerous brew she had concocted.

During the weeks following the brutal battle that had left him badly wounded and his brother dead Enio Gunn had listened to the words of his mother and believed every single one of them. The intoxicating tonic helped the old Cree woman to control his every thought and steer his every action.

She created the demons and filled his hapless mind with them as she had always done. A mind which had never functioned as minds were meant to do was easily manipulated. And when the

49

manipulator was also quite mad it became even easier.

Her hatred had grown over the years. At one time she only hated her own kind: people who had disowned her for falling in love with an albino monster named Axil Gunn. They had cast her out. They had shunned her. As she had grown older and uglier her hatred had spread until everyone was her enemy. A million irrational thoughts had darted through her skull over the decades she had lived in the desert. Her demented imaginings had become real to her. She saw the monsters in everyone and knew that they were all intent on destroying her unless she made her men destroy them first.

Every word she had ever uttered had been twisted by her own broken mind. She above all was responsible for the Phantom in all his incarnations.

Her poison had filled her husband's mind. Soon he had become worse than she, for he turned words of hate into deadly actions. Her sons had then been the ones who had absorbed her continued mission of hate.

Slowly they too began to succumb to the brainwashing of their mother. They had always believed every word she filled their heads with. No God-fearing preacher had ever managed to control his flock as well the Cree woman had managed to do with her own family.

Although the sons had looked the same the elder of the pair had never ventured far away from his mother to emulate his father and brother. That was the reason he had been there on the high mesa when Enio had arrived after slaughtering his way through the desert back to his birthplace. Although the elder Gunn had never sought to seek people to kill, as his father and brother had done, he was as lethal with any form of weaponry as they were. When the shooting had started on the high mountainside he had been no less capable with his guns than his kinfolk. It had been he who had managed to get the drop on the three intruders, not the wounded Enio. Yet he had stopped to gloat too soon, and that had been his final misjudgement.

As children both brothers had witnessed their father losing his battle with Hickok two decades earlier and had vowed to one day avenge Axil Gunn.

Vengeance was a cruel mistress.

Yet Enio Gunn only knew that he had to seek revenge because his mother had pounded it into his mind over and over again until he had grown to think it was his own idea. It had become his only reason to exist. Without hatred there would be no Phantom.

Even with the countless dead left in his wake as he had travelled down from Badwater, Gunn knew that it was Wild Bill Hickok who was his chosen target. His true target. The others he had mercilessly slain were all just bait to lure Hickok back to him.

The Phantom would keep killing until Hickok responded to the gruesome and bloody taunting and returned to face him.

The fearsome figure did not feel the cold as other men with blood in their bodies did. He tore the reins from the tailgate of the large covered wagon, grabbed his saddle horn and mounted the skittish grey. There was no sign of humanity in the lifeless face as he swung the horse abruptly around and rammed his bloodstained spurs into its scarred flanks.

As always it obeyed its master.

Even a horse knew that it did not pay to defy the Phantom. Only death awaited creatures that did.

Gunn thundered away from the mesas into the frost-covered desert. The blue moonlit sand kicked up behind the hoofs of the tall-shouldered animal as the deadly horseman sought new prey.

There was fresh blood to spill.

The rider knew he would find and spill a lot of it long before the sun of a new day rose again. Anyone who got in his way would be killed. Gunn was ready and willing to keep destroying people until Hickok returned. Even though the desert land always appeared to be devoid of life, there was life. There were always plenty of people in the desert and most of them were waiting for death to claim them. But none ever imagined in their darkest nightmares that death rode a grey stallion.

The Phantom spurred on.

4

Tom Dix stared out of the café window as the liverymen backed a fresh six-horse team between the traces and started to buckle the chains. Dix pushed his empty plate into the middle of the chequered tablecloth next to his pal's.

'They washed all the blood off the coach pretty good, Dixie,' Dan remarked as he downed his coffee. He yawned. 'That advance on our wages sure tasted fine.'

Dix stood and adjusted his gunbelt. 'Reckon we'd better head on over to the stagecoach depot. It's nearly ten.'

Dan Shaw rose to his feet. 'I sure wish we could catch up with some sleep rather than have to take that stage out. I'm damn tuckered, pal.'

Dix smiled and lifted his hat off the chair beside him. He placed it on his grey hair. 'A deal's a deal. We promised that Drew critter we'd take the stage out and that's what we gotta do. Look on the bright side: we got us a full belly out of it.'

The pair left the cafe and walked out into the amber lantern-light. They untied their horses' reins from the hitching rail and followed the stagecoach as it was led towards the depot.

'We'll tie our horses to the back of the stage just in case we need them,' Dix said.

Dan gave a slow nod. 'Yep, ya right. I don't reckon it'd make much sense leaving the nags here, considering we don't intend ever coming back.'

Dix tilted his head back. His keen eyesight focused on the boardwalk outside the Overland Stagecoach depot. There were three people standing there, besides Carter Drew.

'It looks like we have a few passengers, Dan.'

'Damn.' Dan sighed. 'I was hoping we were taking an empty coach back to Cactus Flats.'

Dix glanced at his pal. 'Why?'

Dan waved his hand thoughtfully. 'It just seems a lot easier not having passengers to worry about. Especially as we're headed back to where the stage was shot up.'

Dix nodded. 'I hadn't thought about that.'

'If we run into the Phantom we'll have more than enough trouble keeping ourselves alive, let alone them,' Dan said.

The two men reached the stage-coach's tailgate and tied their long leathers to it. Dix lifted his fender and hooked its stirrup over the saddle horn. He uncinched his saddle and dragged it off the horse's back.

Dan watched as his partner tossed the saddle under the canvas of the tailgate. 'I'm not gonna lie to ya, Dixie. I'm troubled about this.'

'You and me both, pal.' Dix helped his friend remove his saddle from his horse and set it beside his own. Dan was breathing heavily as he secured the straps of the canvas tightly.

Both men stepped up on to the boardwalk and accepted the papers that Drew handed them.

'What are these?' Dix wondered.

Drew handed a pencil to Dan and pushed a clipboard under his nose. 'Just sign this.'

Dan licked the pencil, signed and then had the pencil snatched from his hand. He raised his eyebrows and watched the stout Drew walk into the well-illuminated office. Dan trailed him and leaned on a well-varnished counter. 'What are the papers for and what did I just sign, Drew?'

'It's just the manifest,' Drew answered. 'You have three paying passengers en route to Cactus Flats via the way station at Apache Springs. You also have a strong-box which you must deliver to our office at Cactus Flats. You've signed to acknowledge this. OK?'

'I reckon so.' Confused, Dan scratched his ear, then walked back out into the fresh air. He studied the passengers.

Two middle-aged men and a well-dressed woman who looked as though she was roughly thirty were handing their luggage to Dix, who was standing on the front wheel and carefully placing the bags on the roof of the stage.

Gallantly Dan removed his Stetson and opened the coach door. The woman entered and sat down with a polite smile. The two men did not smile. They pushed past the retired lawman and hurriedly climbed into the coach. They sat opposite the young woman. They might have been wearing expensive suits but neither had any manners, Dan Shaw thought.

Dix jumped back down on to the boardwalk as Dan closed the coach door and returned his hat to his head. He smiled and walked along to the lead horses with Dan at his shoulder.

'She sure must be mighty brave to take a stage after what happened earlier, Dixie,' Dan said as his friend checked the harnesses.

Dix grinned at his pal. 'She's real pretty, too.'

'Is she?' Dan cleared his throat. 'I didn't notice.'

Dix squared up to his comrade. 'Sure ya didn't.'

'Which one of us is driving this damn thing and which one of us gets to ride shotgun?' Dan asked as Dix checked every chain and strap linking the sturdy animals to the long traces.

'I'm riding shotgun,' Dix said firmly.

'How come?'

'I'm the only one that can hit what he shoots at, Dan,' Dix reasoned. 'So that makes you the driver.'

Dan shrugged and trailed Dix back to the front wheel of the stage. 'I hate it when ya talk sense, Dixie. I ain't never handled a six-horse team before. Looks a tad tricky.'

'All ya gotta do is aim the lead horses and keep ya boot on the brake pole,' Dix said confidently. 'Them horses look smart enough to stay on the road, though.'

Both men climbed up on to the high driver's board and took their respective positions. The seat was still damp where a lot of soapy water had been used to wash most of the blood from it.

Dan picked up the heavy lengths of rein and tried to work out which of the long leathers was attached to which pair of horses below them.

'This looks complicated, Dixie,' Dan admitted.

Dix checked the scattergun resting at his feet. It was loaded and ready for action. He then checked his trusty pair of Colt .45s. They too were ready for anything the long journey might throw at them.

'We gonna head out any time soon, Dan?' Dix asked, pulling the collar of his jacket up to shield his neck. 'We're too old to waste time.'

'As soon as I figure out what to do first we'll be headed out, Dixie,' Dan told him.

'Just release the brake, slap the reins across them nags and yell out something loud,' Dix suggested. 'How hard can it be?'

Dan Shaw glanced seriously at his friend. 'Do ya figure we'll bump into the Phantom, Dixie? We sure didn't do too well last time. If it hadn't been for Wild Bill we'd be dead.'

'We won't bump into anyone,' Dix said. 'Not if we stay here, anyway.'

The older man nervously released the brake pole and then whipped the horses with the long leathers. The team responded and headed along the narrow street at a steady pace. Dan Shaw beamed triumphantly at his pal.

'This ain't as hard as it looks.'

Dix pointed ahead, then closed his eyes as the horses trotted towards the side of a building. 'If ya get around that corner I'll agree with ya, pard.'

To the alarm of their three passengers half of the coach mounted the board-walk and bounced violently. Dan wrestled with the reins before he eventually managed to get all four wheels back on the street.

'How am I doing?' Dan shouted as he tried to stop the horses from wandering from one side of the street to the other.

Nervously Dix opened one eye. 'I'll tell ya if we manage to get out of town, Dan.'

5

The haunting light of the crescent moon and the scattering of stars bathed the entire desert in a hazy hue. It was the largest graveyard anyone could ever imagine. Icy mist shimmered as though alive. It appeared as if the coming of night had brought the spirits of the desert's countless victims up from their sandy graves to haunt those who still clung to life.

It was an unearthly scene and yet it held no fear for the deadly slaughterer known as the Phantom. For the majority of those who had died in the vast desert had been killed by the creature known as Enio Gunn.

The strange light and chilling cold were exactly as Gunn preferred it. When you had no pigment to protect your flesh you travelled by night. You only lived during the hours of darkness.

The Phantom killed by night.

Gunn knew that his eyes could cope with starlight and even the illumination of a full moon but he was virtually blind during the hours of daylight. The sun was his only true enemy for it tortured him. When he did travel during the daytime it was beneath the protective canvas of his mother's covered wagon. Only the darkness gave him the freedom to strike out at those his demented reasoning considered to be his other enemies. He could never defeat the sun but he could defeat the people who dared enter his land.

Gunn had ridden a straight course across the sand for almost an hour before hauling rein. Dust settled over the horseman and his mount as he studied the area that surrounded him. Where was his prey? Where were the people he wanted to kill?

He had to kill. Kill as many as he could in order to draw the fly into his web. Hickok had to realize that he had failed, that the true Phantom was still alive and still killing.

Gunn inhaled the cold air through his flared nostrils and then gave a sickening chuckle. His honed senses were alerted that he had at last detected someone to kill.

Someone was cooking their supper. Its aroma filled his nose as he steadied his horse and rose up in his stirrups. The gaunt figure balanced like a tightrope walker for a few seconds as he sniffed the night air. Then he tilted his head, pushed his mane of white hair off his face and squinted hard from behind his black glass spectacles.

Being an albino had its advantages during the darkest of nights, one of which was being able to see perfectly in almost total darkness. The blackest of nights were no protection for the innocent from Gunn's keen eyesight. There was nowhere for any of his victims to hide.

None of those who had tasted the wrath of the albino rider had ever had any reason to think they were in danger until it was too late. Gunn killed without motive or reason apart from the insane pleasure it gave him.

It has always been totally impossible for anyone to protect themselves from crazed men who desire to kill simply because they can.

The ragged rocks he had ridden from were behind him but a mile ahead of his grey stallion was a more impressive mountain range. One he knew like the back of his colourless hand. Five miles to his right were the caves he and his mother had left only days earlier.

Straight ahead of his horse's nose stood a high column of rock, which looked like a finger pointing up to heaven. It towered over the rest of the mountain range. Gunn knew there were more caves there. Caves which had at one time been mined for the gold ore some of them contained.

The creature lowered himself back down on the saddle and started to nod. His nostrils had picked up the aroma of cooking but it was his eyes that had spotted the distant glow of a campfire.

'There ya are,' Gunn whispered to himself. 'Keep cooking ya grub and I'll have me no trouble finding ya.'

The Phantom spurred and drove his grey across the frost-covered sand towards his next unsuspecting victims. There might only be one man to kill out there by the campfire, but to Gunn it was just the start of what he hoped would prove to be a long night of slaughtering.

The closer he got to the distant flames the stronger the scent of bacon grew in his nostrils.

Enio Gunn rammed his spurs back and felt the powerful stallion respond by finding new speed. There was a terror in the large grey horse. A terror that it tried vainly to outrun but the spurs continued to draw blood.

Dust kicked up from the animal's hoofs as the grey tore towards its ruthless master's next victim. The sound of the pounding echoed all around the charging horse and rider. It was like the noise of an Apache war drum, signalling the coming of death.

With every stride of the horse's long legs the infamous Phantom closed the distance between themselves and the glowing fire set close to the rocks and the tall rock column. Gunn could smell the bacon as it fried in the distant skillet. It grew more powerful with each beat of his merciless heart, yet it was not the scent of the cooking food that was making the Phantom drool as he forced his horse on.

It was the thought of another fresh kill that excited him. Soon every sinew in his ghostlike body would be rejoicing as he killed another unsuspecting man. His mind was almost feverish as the thought engulfed him.

He spurred harder.

He could see the fire clearly now through his black glass spectacles. It flickered and danced in the frosty air ahead of him. Sparks drifted upward and danced like fireflies. The flames were like a curled finger enticing him towards it.

Again he rose in his stirrups and leaned over the neck of the charging stallion. Gunn could see two men bathed in the red glow of the campfire.

One stood, then so did the other. The noise of the hoofbeats filled their ears. Their curious naïve souls wondered who apart from themselves was out in the middle of the desert at this time of night. They were here because, like many prospectors before them, the desire to find gold had lured them to this inhospitable place.

Both men squinted towards the mist. They could hear but not see the unexpected visitor, but neither man was concerned. Like so many others they could not comprehend danger even when it was heading right for them.

Then the frosty haze lifted and they got their first glimpse of the rider. At first they thought it was a trick of the eerie starlight. Then, as the horseman closed in on them they realized that this was no ordinary rider. The fearsome white face became clear in the light of their fire. Neither had ever seen anything like it before.

The long white beard and the flowing mane of hair were unusual enough, but then the two men focused on the colourless face of Enio Gunn. It was like looking at a ghost on horseback. A ghost with a gun in its free hand.

For a moment both men were unable to move. They were so frightened that neither seemed to be able to do anything apart from stare at the hideous creature who was riding towards them.

'What the hell is that?' the older of the two men asked as he held the skillet in his shaking hand.

'Damned if I know,' the other man answered.

'It looks like them stories of the Phantom.'

'I heard tell he was dead.'

The man holding the skillet swallowed hard. 'Whatever that is it sure ain't dead.'

The realization that they were in mortal danger suddenly swept over them. The first man dropped the skillet, turned and started to run for his rifle.

The other was soon on his heels.

The Phantom charged across the sand astride his snorting grey stallion and laughed as he watched them rush to where their Winchesters were resting against a boulder.

It was too late though.

Before the two men had reached the rifles Gunn had already cocked the hammer of his Colt. He dragged his reins to one side, then aimed and fired. A deafening flash cut through the cold air. The first man was punched off his feet by the impact of the deadly bullet, which hit him in his back. He crashed into the ground. His fingers clawed at the sand but he was still ten feet away from his rifle.

Then Gunn cocked his gun again, stretched his arm to its full length and squeezed its trigger.

Another blast echoed around the desert. The second running man staggered and then fell forward limply

72

on to his face. No heart was strong enough to take a bullet.

Gunn stopped his horse and looked down at them. He dismounted and walked between the two men on the sand and studied his handiwork. The groaning of the man close to the rifles caught his attention. The Phantom cocked his smoking gun a third time and walked to where the first man was still scraping at the sand with his fingers.

'Why ain't ya dead?' Gunn growled.

The wounded man was shaking as blood encircled him. He managed to raise himself up on one elbow and stare in horror at the unholy figure that loomed over his helpless body.

'Who are ya?' the man asked. 'What ya do this for?'

The Phantom did not answer.

He simply aimed at the man's head and fired. The bullet shattered the prospector's skull into a hundred fragments. Gore splattered around the body. As if nothing had happened the Phantom slid his .45 into its holster and walked towards the campfire.

Gunn reached the skillet resting on the edge of the ashes and looked down at the uneaten supper. He bent down, plucked the bacon from its blackened pan and forced it into his mouth. As he chewed the burnt bacon, grease ran down his white beard and dripped on to his blood-covered boots.

He swallowed.

It was hungry work killing folks, he thought. Gunn licked his fingers, then grabbed his reins. He tugged until his grey mount drew closer to him again. Gunn held the saddle horn, stepped into the stirrup and eased his long colourless form back on to his saddle.

He gave a sickening laugh and then turned the horse to face the desert he had just galloped across. The cold haze moved just above its freezing surface, but Gunn did not see it. All he could see was the crude trail that cut through the middle of the otherwise pristine sand. It went on endlessly in both directions. A thought occurred to Gunn. Soon there would be another stagecoach travelling through the desert carrying more potential victims.

His eyes darted back to the bodies.

Two dead men were not enough, his demented brain told him over and over again. He had to add to the tally. There had to be even more dead. There had to be more victims of the Phantom if he were to achieve his goal.

A crude plan festered in his mind. If he were to let the world know that the Phantom was still living, he would have to paint his name on the next stage-coach he attacked. He had to paint the name of the Phantom in blood.

The news would spread like a forest fire. It would not take long for everyone within a hundred miles to start mumbling his name in terror.

Then Hickok would come.

He had to come.

Wild Bill Hickok would then pay for what he had done.

Pay with his life.

Gunn spurred again. The grey stallion thundered back across the frost-covered sand. Its master was in search of more people to destroy. He was headed towards the stagecoach trail.

The night was still young and the Phantom was still eager to add to his tally of victims.

6

The high-shouldered thoroughbred appaloosa mare moved through the starlight slowly as its reins were gently teased by its equally impressive master. Its silver-embossed saddle livery glinted in the torchlight as the rider approached the remote way station's high walls. Apache Springs was like a small fortress set in the heart of the desert. It was a glinting jewel in an otherwise barren landscape. An oasis.

It had remained virtually the same since monks had discovered its precious spring water and built a monastery around it. Only the stone cross had gone but the adobe structures, which had originally been cells and stables, remained. A few structural adaptations had turned the abandoned house of God into a valuable asset for the stagecoach company. A much-needed outpost where people and beasts could find food, water and rest before the long cruel trek to Rio Hondo.

The high walls that surrounded the building and courtyard of the way station had been there for more than a century, but it had been a long time since they had been truly needed.

At first they had provided protection from Apache attacks and then from those who might decide to try and rob the vulnerable stagecoaches as they travelled through the otherwise lawless territory.

The way station was a sanctuary. A safe haven in an untamed region. Rance Howard had been the stationmaster for nearly two years and had almost quit a few months earlier when the killing had started. The thought of there being a creature calling himself the Phantom had chilled Howard worse than the desert night air.

Howard had never been a man to live by the guns he was obliged to wear around his hips. He had always preferred his excitement to be literary. He had read every dime novel he had managed to get his hands on. When the Phantom had come within spitting distance of his way station Howard had briefly thought it was time to quit and find himself an easier, safer occupation.

All that had changed when his hero, Wild Bill Hickok, had unexpectedly disembarked from a stage and decided to stay for a few days. Those brief moments when the legendary man of numerous dime novels had spoken to Howard had taught the young station manager more than all of his years of living had previously done. Suddenly Howard had realized that however tall the tales of the reputed exploits of his hero seemed in the well-thumbed books he treasured, the real man was no less colourful.

When he had witnessed how Hickok and his two friends had ridden off to find the Phantom, Howard knew what true courage meant. Many are called brave but real acts of bravery are when someone risks his own life for no better reason than that it is the right thing to do. Hickok might have become a shadow of his former self but he still had that spark of courage few men ever discover within themselves.

That had been months earlier and the desert had been quiet ever since Hickok's departure. Howard knew that the three men who had ridden out from his station that night must have succeeded where so many others had failed.

Howard sucked on his cigarette as he rested his shoulder against a porch upright outside the station's main building. The clear sky was filled with countless stars. It reminded the young man of the last time he had seen the tall man with the long brown hair and the unique holster which allowed its owner to cross-draw his weapons at an unbelievable speed. Then as smoke drifted from his mouth Howard noticed one of his men on the eastern parapet waving across the darkness at him.

'We got us a rider heading in, Rance.'

Howard dropped his cigarette on to the sand and crushed it underfoot before he raced across the courtyard and made his way up to where Shorty McCabe was standing beneath one of the station's fiery torches. Shorty aimed his rifle barrel out into the gloom and leaned closer to his boss.

'There,' Shorty said. 'Can ya see him, Rance?'

Howard bit his lip and screwed up his tired eyes. He stared hard into the swirling mist that hid the horseman from view.

'Are ya sure there's someone there?' Howard asked. Then he too spotted the rider. 'Hold on. I see something. Ya right. It is a rider.'

'He's riding slow,' Shorty said. 'That nag is barely walking. Who in tarnation could it be?'

'Can ya make him out, Shorty?' Howard asked. He leaned on the white-washed wall. 'Can ya?'

'Nope,' Shorty replied from the

corner of his mouth. 'But I can sure see his fancy saddle.'

Howard balanced on his wrists as far out as he dared from the high wall. Then he smiled. 'It can't be. Why'd he wanna come back here?'

Shorty looked at his boss. 'Ya recognize the critter, Rance?'

'I sure do.' Howard beamed and slapped his holstered gun. 'Ya know who that critter is? Do ya, Shorty?'

The smaller man shook his head slowly. 'Whoever he is he sure is mighty fancy. That buckskin coat he's wearing must have cost him a pretty penny, let alone all that silver he got tacked to his saddle. Must have cost him a fortune.'

Howard grabbed the shoulders of his impressed employee and shook him. 'That just happens to be the one and only Wild Bill Hickok, Shorty.'

'It is?' Shorty looked again as the horseman rode into the torchlight. 'He sure needs a haircut.'

Howard smiled and patted the smaller man's cheek. 'I'd not mention that to him, Shorty. He gets kinda ornery when folks comment on his appearance. I'd hate to lose a good liveryman like you.'

Shorty watched as his boss ran back down the steps to the courtyard and towards the east gate. As was their daily ritual the station workers secured both the gates as soon as the sun set.

Excitedly, Rance Howard lifted the hefty lump of wood from its metal braces and dropped it on the sand. He pulled one of the large doors open and watched as the appaloosa mare was reined in. The torchlight danced across horse and master as the hooded eyes of the rider stared from beneath his hat brim at the station manager.

'Mr Hickok.' Howard smiled in greeting.

Wild Bill removed his broad-brimmed Stetson from his mane of long dark hair and held it across his heart.

'Howdy, Rance,' Hickok acknowledged.

'What ya doing back here in Apache Springs?' Howard asked, running to the horse as its master returned his hat to his head. 'I'd have thought ya would have found someplace better than here to visit.'

'Apache Springs ain't so bad, Rance,' Hickok said. He slowly dismounted from the magnificent horse and handed the reins to the station manager. 'Besides, I got myself some business I have to finish off.'

Howard led the mare into the station grounds as the tall figure strode next to him. 'I thought you'd finished ya business in these parts, Wild Bill. Ya did kill the Phantom after all.'

Hickok paused inside the courtyard and took off his beaded gauntlets and pushed them into the pockets of his buckskin jacket.

'I'm through killing, Rance,' the elegant man muttered in a low tone. 'That kinda business ain't too profitable.'

The station manager looked at the man who, even in his trail gear, looked better dressed than most other men he had ever encountered. 'Then what kinda business are ya talking about, Bill?'

'The business I'm best at, Rance,' Hickok replied. He pulled a long cigar from a silver case, bit off its tip then pushed it through his drooping moustache into the corner of his mouth. 'I've got card-playing business to do. A real serious game of poker to win. If I do win I'll be set for what's left of my life.'

'Where's the game being held?' Howard asked curiously. 'Rio Hondo? I hear they got a real big gaming hall there.'

'Nope. Not Rio Hondo.' Hickok picked up the large length of wood and secured the gate again for his friend. 'Apache Springs.'

'Here?' Howard looked at the elegant figure standing in his trail gear. 'Ya gonna have a game of poker here?'

Hickok nodded and struck a match. 'Yep.'

'I don't understand, Wild Bill.' Howard scratched his neck thoughtfully. 'Who the hell are ya gonna play poker with here?'

James Butler Hickok cupped the flame of his match against the night chill and raised it to the end of his cigar. Before he lit it his hooded eyes glared at the station manager.

'There's three real well-heeled gamblers on their way here from Cactus Flats on the stage, Rance. This is a real high-stakes game. Winner takes all no matter how long it takes. When they arrive the game starts,' Hickok said. 'This is a ten thousand dollar per player game.'

Amazed, Howard looked across the courtyard as his other liveryman, Luke Stevens, ambled towards them. 'Take Mr. Hickok's horse into the stable, Luke.'

The famed gambler watched as the liveryman did as he was told and took hold of the reins. Stevens smiled when he recognized Hickok.

'Nice to see ya again, Wild Bill.'

'And you, Luke. Look after that mare. She's young and like all young females she's got vinegar.' Hickok tossed a silver dollar at Stevens. 'Treat her kindly.'

'I'll treat her like she was my own, Wild Bill,' Stevens said over his shoulder. He led the appaloosa towards the stable.

Hickok walked towards the main building inside the station's courtyard. Smoke drifted over his shoulder. Howard trailed Hickok to where lanterns hung on the porch close to the station's main door. Hickok exhaled a long line of smoke at the ground, then looked around the familiar surroundings. 'I like it here. Kinda peaceful.'

'Ya holding the game here?' The station manager repeated his question.

'Yep.' Hickok nodded as his hooded eyes studied the face of the younger man. 'Ya ain't got a problem with that, have ya, Rance? I picked this place because it's remote. Last big-money game of poker I was in was at Dodge. Guns started being drawn and fired. That's the trouble with high stakes. It draws the vermin out of the woodwork something awful. I figured if there was any gunplay here nobody will know and we can always bury the dead cheats in the desert out yonder. Does that bother you?'

The taller man wrapped an arm around Howard's shoulder and gave it a powerful squeeze. The way station manager could feel the strength of the famed gunfighter.

'It don't bother me none.' Howard shrugged nervously. 'But I just work here. I don't make the rules, Wild Bill.'

'The stagecoach company will never know,' Hickok said in a soothing tone. 'The game could be over in a matter of hours. Hell, the longest it could last would only be a few days.'

'Days?' Rance Howard was torn as to what he should do for the best. There was his loyalty to his employers and there was the respect he had for his lifelong hero. 'I ain't sure the company rules allow gambling here, Wild Bill.'

Hickok grinned from behind his

drooping moustache. 'Then we won't tell them. What they don't know about they sure can't fret over, can they? That's settled then.'

Howard knew there was nobody else he would ever have allowed to break company rules. Only Hickok.

'Reckon so, Wild Bill.' Howard nodded. 'Ya did rid the desert of the Phantom after all, and stopped all the killing that was happening in these parts. Reckon the company owes ya a big debt. Ya right. You've earned the right to play a friendly game of poker.'

'I knew ya had vinegar, Rance.' Hickok inhaled on his cigar and strode into the main room of the station. His eyes darted at the centre of the room to the large table. He walked towards it.

Hickok stopped next to the long table and ran a hand over its surface. 'This'll do just fine.'

The earlier words concerning the last high-stakes poker game Hickok had participated in troubled the manager. He rubbed his neck and tried to catch the long-haired man's attention.

'What did ya mean when ya was talking about cheats and gunplay, Bill?' Howard enquired. 'I don't like the idea of you boys shooting it out in here. Especially if'n there happens to be passengers eating their grub. I'd get in a heap of trouble if anyone got shot.'

'Don't get all lathered up.' Hickok tapped the ash from his cigar and returned it to his mouth. 'It's mighty doubtful there'll be any shooting in here.'

'What did ya mean about cheats?'

The hooded eyes looked at Howard. 'Listen up. Cheats usually get caught and then the shooting starts. Sometimes in a crowded gambling hall or saloon the cheats have folks working with them, ready to help their *amigos*. This is a quiet way station. There'll just be the four of us. No back-shooters to worry about.'

'How can ya tell if someone is cheating?'

'Hell. It takes one to know one,

Rance.' Hickok took the cigar from his mouth and winked. 'If someone plays an ace and you've already palmed that same card and have it tucked up ya sleeve, that means they're cheating. Don't it?'

Rance Howard nodded. 'Yeah.'

'Ya let them know that you've noticed they're cheating and then if they don't back down you kill 'em.' Hickok patted his guns. 'Most right-minded critters look at these and they know the odds of them living to tell the tale ain't too good.'

Howard sighed heavily and wondered whether he had made the right decision. It was too late now, though, to change his mind and he knew it.

'I imagine it will be a nice peaceful game between friends and nothing bad will happen. I'm sure of it.'

'Any chance of a meal?' Hickok asked. 'I'm plumb hungry with all this gabbing.'

Howard sighed. 'That's a real sore point, Wild Bill. Our cook quit last week. I'm expecting a new one any time though.'

'I sure hope he arrives damn soon, Rance. I'm hungry enough to chew on saddle leather,' Hickok said.

Suddenly the walls of the large room resounded as the unmistakable noise of pistol and rifle fire filled the ears of the two men.

'That came from the wall, Rance,' Hickok announced knowingly.

'Shorty!' Howard gasped. 'He's being attacked.'

Swiftly Hickok drew one of his guns, cocked its hammer and turned. The tall, lean man ran out into the lantern-light with the way station manager at his side. Hickok paused, spat his cigar at the sand and looked up towards the parapet near the east gate just as a volley of gunshots rang out. Shorty fired his rifle again out into the darkness. Then another half-dozen gunshots were returned.

Both Hickok and Howard watched in stunned horror as the small, sturdy liveryman buckled, dropped his rifle and then fell from his high perch.

The thud of his body hitting the frost-covered sand filled the night air. It was a sickening sound.

7

'Shorty!' Howard gasped in shock. He ran towards the place where he had seen Shorty land. A mere step behind him Hickok moved with his gun held firmly in his right hand. Upon reaching the motionless Shorty on the ground Howard knelt down. Hickok did not stop. He continued on towards the steps. His long legs mounted the steps two at a time until he reached the parapet.

Red-hot tapers cut through the night air. Hickok was forced to duck. He fired his gun blindly at a target he could not see. The mist, which had only been a few feet above the frost-covered sand when he arrived at Apache Springs, was now a dense fog. A fog which was high enough to hide the horseman who kept shooting at the high parapet. Bullets ricocheted off the adobe wall, showering the crouching Hickok in dust.

Hickok shook the spent casings from his smoking gun and reloaded. Another few shots came from out of the mist. Two hit the top of the whitewashed wall again as another passed within inches of the tall man's left shoulder. Then the shooting stopped. Hickok stared out into the strange, starlit desert. His hooded eyes vainly searched for the gunman. All he could hear was the snorting of a horse somewhere in the mist.

'Show yourself, damn it!' Hickok snarled quietly. His finger stroked his gun's trigger. 'Give me a target and I'll kill ya.'

'Who the hell's out there, Wild Bill?' Howard called up from where he was kneeling. 'Who shot Shorty?'

Hickok did not reply. He was listening hard, trying to hear his target so that he could take another shot. All he needed was a target and he would fan his gun hammer until all six of his bullets had exploded into action.

But only an eerie silence greeted his ears. Whoever it was out there was keeping just far enough away from the station walls for its blazing torches not to betray his position.

'Who was it, Bill?' Howard yelled out again.

Before Hickok could reply he heard the sound of hoofs beating a retreat on top of the frosty desert sand somewhere out in the darkness. Within a few heart-beats the noise had faded into the swirling icy fog and he knew his chance had gone.

'Damn it all!' Hickok raged.

'Can ya see who it is, Wild Bill?' the distraught Howard shouted out once more.

'If I could I'd have killed the son of a bitch, boy,' Hickok yelled back. Angrily he rose back to his full height. He released his gun hammer and eased it back down against the body of his gun. He then holstered it.

'Who the hell's out there?' Howard asked. He watched Hickok rise to his feet and turn back to the top of the steps.

'Nobody now.' The tall man raced

down the steps and stood looking down at the injured liveryman. 'Whoever it was he's high-tailed it.'

Howard was confused. 'Who'd be shooting at someone like Shorty?'

The cannier Hickok shook his head. 'Whoever it was doing the shooting out there seemed to just want to kill folks. Folks who happened to be on the wall. Easy pickings. If you'd bin up there that varmint would have shot you instead. It just don't make any sense.'

Howard rested a hand on the bleeding wound in Shorty's chest as he carefully checked for broken bones. 'He don't seem to have broken any bones.'

'Ya mean he ain't dead?' Hickok was surprised.

'Not yet anyway,' Howard answered. 'Give me a hand. We gotta get him inside. I'll put him in one of the empty passenger rooms out back.'

'You get the room ready, Rance.' Hickok crouched, slid one hand under Shorty's neck and the other under his knees. He then stood back up with the small man cradled in his arms.

Rance raced to the main building as Luke Stevens came out of the stables holding a rifle in his arms.

'What happened, Rance?'

'Shorty's bin shot. Get up on the walls and keep a look-out, Luke,' Howard ordered. He entered the building, Hickok following with the unconscious Shorty in his arms.

Howard opened the door nearest to the main room and then struck a match. He lit the coal tar lamp and adjusted its flame until the room was filled with light. Hickok entered close behind him and lay the wounded man down on the sheets of the bed.

'Get some boiling water, Rance,' Hickok said. He removed his buckskin coat and threw it across the room at a chair. He rolled up his sleeves. 'I got a bullet to cut out of this little man.'

Howard nodded. Just as he reached the open doorway he paused for a moment and looked at Hickok.

'Who was that out there, Bill?' he

asked nervously. 'Who shot him?'

Hickok stared at the younger man. There was no hint of expression in his face. 'Get that boiling water fast, Rance. I reckon I can save this critter's bacon if I can find that lump of lead and cut it out. Now move.'

The way station manager did as he was instructed. He raced to the kitchen area, where a large kettle sat atop a flame on the oven range. His mind raced as he carefully filled a bowl with the boiling liquid.

What was happening?

Why had the station been attacked?

Who had attacked it?

And why?

There were so many questions and not a single answer. He felt sick to his stomach. Then his young eyes caught a glimpse of a clock set high on the whitewashed wall.

It was nearly midnight. The Rio Hondo-bound stage from Cactus Flats was due at any time, Howard thought. What if it ran into the same gunman who had attacked the station?

He lifted the bowl filled with boiling water and ventured back towards the room where Hickok waited with a long stiletto in his hands. Howard placed the bowl carefully down on a table close to the bed and Hickok dropped his knife into it.

'Help me get his damn coat and shirt off, Rance,' Hickok said in a low whisper. 'I gotta find skin before I can start digging.'

Then from somewhere out in the desert both men heard another volley of desperate shooting erupt. Both men looked at one another.

'That rider must have come back, Bill.'

Hickok shook his head. 'That shooting is a mile or so away, Rance. He's found something else to attack out in the desert. Don't pay it no mind, boy. We got us a life to save here and that's a tad more important than us shooting it out with no locobean.'

More distant shots filled their ears.

Hickok dropped the blood-soaked clothing on the floor, then ripped the long johns apart to reveal the hideous bullet hole in Shorty's flesh. The continuous shooting was starting to anger Hickok.

'That shooting is making my cutting hand a tad jumpy, Rance,' he admitted as he pulled the long-bladed knife from the bowl and shook it dry. 'Get out there and help Luke kill whoever it is doing all that shooting. I need me a steady hand here.'

The station manager suddenly remembered what it was that had occurred to him when he looked at the clock in the station kitchen.

'The stage!' Howard gasped.

Hickok looked at the station manager. 'What?'

'That's what he's shooting at, Bill,' Howard reasoned. 'He's attacking the damn stage. It's due here at any time from Cactus Flats. That must be it.'

'The stage?' Hickok repeated as he slid the long thin blade of his knife into the flesh of the unconscious Shorty. His hooded eyes burned into the station manager. 'What ya standing there for, Rance?'

'What ya mean, Bill?'

'Get going, Rance. Ya gotta stop that bastard, damn it.' Hickok snorted. 'I got me three wealthy card-players on that stage coming here for me to pluck like turkeys on the Fourth of July. Grab a rifle and give that stage cover. Hell. I could lose me a fortune.'

The younger man nodded and ran from the room.

Howard grabbed a rifle from the wall rack in the main room and ran as fast as his legs would take him out of the building and out into the courtyard. The distant shooting continued to resound around the walls of the station as Howard raced towards the east gate. As he ran he could see Luke Stevens staring out into the mist with his carbine clutched in his hands. The young manager did not stop running until he was standing next to Stevens on top of the parapet. He sucked in icy air and rested a hand on the livery-man's shoulder.

'Can ya see anything, Luke?'

Stevens aimed his rifle barrel at the rocks on the rise a mile across the desert sand. Even the mist and the dim starlight could not hide the flashes of gunfire from the eyes of both men.

'There sure is a hell of a lot of shooting going on out there. It kinda sounds and looks like there's a storm heading towards the station, Rance,' the liveryman muttered as his strong hands gripped his Winchester firmly.

'There is, Luke,' Howard said grimly. 'A real bad storm by my reckoning.'

'I ain't scared of no bushwhacking critter,' Stevens snorted angrily. 'I'm ready to chew on a tornado if that's what it takes to stop the varmint that shot Shorty. I'm riled, Rance. Mighty riled.'

'Good. Now get ready to kill whoever it is attacking the stage, Luke,' Howard said, cranking the rifle in his own hands.

A spent casing flew from the magazine of the rifle as Stevens cranked his weapon's hand guard.

'You bet.'

8

The boulders flashed as lightning rods
of lethal lead spewed from the barrels
of the weapons of the stagecoach guard
and the deadly rider who was attacking
it. The narrow confines of the canyon
intensified the deafening gunfire. The
speeding stagecoach carrying the three
wealthy card-players from Cactus Flats
rocked back and forth as its driver tried
desperately to reach the way station
before one of its attacker's bullets found
its target. The rough ground was in
total contrast to the rest of the trail that
separated the distant town and Apache
Springs. Years earlier dynamite had
cleared the route through the small
outcrop of rocks from the desert that
dominated the region. The trail was just
wide enough to allow the width of a
stagecoach to navigate through the
rocks.

It had provided a place for the devilish Phantom to hide and await the unsuspecting stagecoach; it had also allowed the skilled driver to keep the villainous Gunn behind his vulnerable vehicle.

The shotgun guard, Travis Smith, had crawled across the roof of the stage and was stretched out between the bags and trunks as the awesome albino horseman raced after the fleeing stagecoach. The darkness lit up each time the deafening shots cut through the air. Smith gripped his smoking Winchester and kept firing vainly at the elusive rider who had appeared out of the mist like the Phantom he believed himself to be. Clouds of dust billowed up from the wheels of the long vehicle as Smith continued to fend off the determined horseman who chased them.

Chunks of wood were ripped from the back of the stagecoach as Gunn's bullets searched for the defiant guard. The chase had only started a few minutes earlier but already the desert night stank of gunsmoke.

The six lathered-up horses galloped down through the rocks and on to the vast, untamed desert plain as Joe Hayes, the seasoned driver, used every ounce of his experience to keep ahead of their pursuer.

Inside the bone-shaking coach the three gamblers held on to anything they could grab hold of. Only one of their number had decided to try and help the guard in fending off their attacker. Long Island Louis was a gambler who had made his fortune playing stud poker better than any other man living west of the Mississippi, but he had not forgotten how to use the guns he always sported. Louis leaned out of the coach window and fired his Remington .44s in turn through the mist and wheel dust as his companions, Jack West and Philo Chance, remained crouched on the floor of the speeding coach in prayer.

Yet so far none of the dozens of bullets that had been fired had found a target.

Thundering in hot pursuit with guns blazing, Enio Gunn had no idea that the man he had vowed to kill was in fact inside the way station that he had attacked only ten minutes earlier. The deranged slaughterer of so many innocent souls had no concept that one of his bullets had actually come within inches of hitting the famed Wild Bill Hickok as the gunfighter had knelt on the way station wall's high parapet.

All Gunn could think of was the stagecoach ahead of him and the potential victims he might be able to add to his bloody tally. A tally he believed would lure Hickok back into the desert once again. Shot after shot came from the smoking hot barrels of his .45s as Gunn steered his grey stallion with his thin but powerful legs and the bloody spurs buckled to his boots.

The stagecoach veered down the trail from the highest point among the rocks towards the desert and the flaming torches that he could see through the high swirling mist.

The muscular Joe Hayes stood in the driver's box with his heavy leathers in his gloved hands and screamed encouragement to the team of charging horses. Few other men in his profession could have kept the stagecoach upright at the speed at which he was forcing his team to travel, but Hayes was no ordinary driver.

In his time he had driven most things with a natural skill that had made him the Overland Stagecoach company's highest-paid employee. This night he was being forced to earn every cent of it.

Lashing the reins down across the backs of the lathered-up horses, Hayes guided them down through a gully of rock and sand, then hauled his reins back. The entire body of the coach shook as its wheels negotiated the uneven surface of the rocky terrain.

Hayes could feel the coach beneath him tilt up on to only two of its wheels before crashing back down and righting itself as the fearless driver forced the team through a gap in the rocks barely wider than the breadth of the sturdy horses. It had worked. The cloud of choking dust that the coach's slight deviation off the road had stirred up had done its job.

For a few moments the blinded horseman behind them was forced to haul his reins up to his chest. He was eating dust and trying to see where the stagecoach had gone.

Hayes had bought them a few precious moments when their attacker's bullets could not find them.

The Phantom had lost sight of his prey.

By the time the choking dust had fallen down into the blinding mist the stagecoach had managed to get within 200 yards of the way station.

The flaming torches high on the way station's walls flickered in the night chill, as if beckoning the stagecoach to it like a moth to a naked flame.

There was safety behind those sturdy

walls and Joe Hayes knew it. All he had to do was cross that 200 yards of exposed sand and drive his stagecoach through the gates. The horses thundered forward through the ice-cold mist as the reins kept lashing down across their backs.

Hayes called out at the top of his voice to the two men he could see standing on its parapet. They had to open the gates, he kept telling himself, as Smith continued to fire his rifle from the back of the stagecoach rooftop. He knew that he dare not slow or stop his team or the ambusher would strike. He had to keep the horses galloping even if it meant crashing through the gates.

'Open them damn gates,' Hayes shouted feverishly over and over again. 'Open them gates.'

Then suddenly through the haze Gunn appeared with one of his reloaded Colts in his raised hand. The gruesome figure steadied his grey stallion, then gave out a raging yell of anguish.

The unearthly cry echoed off rocks as the rider glared with fiery eyes at the fleeing stage. He saw one of the men on the walls of the station disappear, then he heard the gates creaking as they were being opened.

The Phantom rammed his gun into its holster and dragged his rifle from its scabbard under his saddle. He swung the long Winchester until its chamber had been activated. The lethal albino raised the rifle and pressed its wooden stock into his shoulder.

Gunn looked down its length through the sights and fired.

The fiery plume of smoke raced from the barrel of the repeating rifle. The bullet left a hot taper in the air as it hit the guard on the stagecoach roof. Even the darkness could not hide the plume of crimson gore which exploded over the bags on top of the stage as it raced into the way station's courtyard.

Gunn cranked the guard, cocked its mechanism again and spat at the sand. He stared back through the raised sights and squeezed its trigger again. Even from where the grey stallion was standing the sound of Luke Stevens screaming in agony could be heard. The Phantom watched as the liveryman toppled over the high whitewashed wall and slid down it until he crashed into the desert sand.

Gunn gave a satisfied grunt. The sight of the bloodstain that marked the outer wall of the way station pleased the lethal horseman. His icy stare matched the temperature as he watched one of the men hastily drag Stevens's body back inside the station's walls.

The gates closed and were secured.

He had managed to kill two of them, his deranged mind told him. Two more to add to his tally of victims.

The Phantom glanced at the sky. It told him things that most men would never be able to comprehend. It told him that he had to start back for the distant caves now. There was no time to waste.

To a creature who had been raised in

the barren wastes of the desert the night sky was like a book he had learned to read long ago. He knew how long it would take him to ride back to the safety of the cool dark caves.

There was no more time to continue killing, Gunn thought. The sky was changing and that meant soon the sun would rise again.

Gunn feared no living man but he feared the rays of the sun and knew what those rays could do to flesh which had no pigment in it to protect it.

His eyes surveyed the way station's gates, which had been closed behind the stagecoach.

'When I come back,' Gunn vowed, 'I'll kill the whole bunch of ya.'

He swung his mount and then spurred.

The Phantom rose in his stirrups and aimed the grey at the dark outline that caressed the star-filled sky. The mountain range peppered with caves awaited, like the old Cree woman, his return.

9

It was hot and getting hotter with every stride of the six-horse stagecoach team. There was no mercy in the morning sun, which beat down on the desert sand. The blinding rays of the reflected light caused both Dix and Dan to shield their eyes as they forged ahead. Both men felt as though they were heading not just into a desert but into Satan's lair. This was a place made in the image of Hell itself.

After nearly freezing during the hours of darkness, now they were being baked alive by the unrelenting sun. Yet there was no turning back. The two men seated on top of the driver's board realized that they were committed.

They had been travelling throughout the night from Rio Hondo towards Apache Springs. Driver Dan Shaw was tired as he felt his pal's elbow nudge his ribs.

'What?' Dan growled.

'There.' Dix pointed.

Dan glanced through the heat haze. 'What ya pointing at?'

'See the flag?' Dix asked.

'All I see is sand, Dixie.' Dan shrugged as he kept the reins patting down on the backs of the team. 'A whole lot of sand. What do you see?'

Dix lifted his Winchester and aimed its barrel at a large boulder set in an ocean of sand. 'Don't ya recall Drew telling us about the water stop? There's the flag. See it?'

The night's frost was evaporating off the dunes of sand ahead of the stagecoach as its lathered-up horses kept obeying Dan's gentle encouragement. Dan leaned forward and then he spotted the flag hanging limply from its pole.

'About time. I reckon these horses must be damn thirsty after dragging this coach all night,' Dan said. 'It's a shame there ain't no wells around here.'

'The nearest springs are at the way

station, Dan,' Dix said, watching his pal steer the team towards the flagpole. 'That's why they keep a water wagon out here for the stages.'

Dan nodded. 'I got me a feeling them passengers will be mighty thankful to be able to stretch their legs.'

'I will as well, pard.'

As Dan guided the stagecoach towards the pole Dix leaned down from his high perch and looked into the interior of the coach. The woman looked in better shape than her two travelling companions.

'We'll be stopping for about fifteen minutes, folks,' Dix told them. 'Ya can stretch ya legs and all.'

Dan's hefty boot pushed down on the brake pole. The stagecoach came to a gentle halt beside the water wagon, which sported the company name painted across its side. Just behind the wagon stood a crude outhouse with two bags of lime propped against its side.

Dix climbed down to the ground and with one hand resting upon a gun grip studied the area. It was as silent as the grave. He moved to the stagecoach door and opened it. Dan descended, walked to the water wagon and started to fill buckets for the horses.

'Here we are, folks,' Dix said.

The two male passengers hurried out of the stagecoach and made their way to the outhouse. The older of the pair entered the privy first. Dix raised an eyebrow and held his hand out to the young woman.

'May I help ya down, ma'am?' he asked politely.

She accepted his hand and carefully made her way through the narrow doorway.

'Thank you,' she said with a genuine smile. 'At least there are two gentlemen on this trip.'

Dix grinned and released her small hand. He glanced at her fellow travellers. 'They ain't exactly full of manners.'

She nodded. 'An understatement.'

Dix removed his hat and ran his

sleeve across his brow. 'I hope ya not regretting this trip, ma'am. It sure is a rough one and no mistake.'

She looked kindly at Dix. 'It's one I'm making through necessity, not choice.'

'My name's Dix. Tom Dix, and that handsome devil watering the team is my old trail pal Dan Shaw. He used to be a lawman before I led him astray. Folks call me Dixie, by the way.'

'Dixie.' She smiled. It was a handsome smile. 'My name happens to be Frances. Frances Ward. Miss Frances Ward.'

Dix looked at her hard. Suddenly in the light of a new day he saw things he had not noticed the night before. Her clothing was clean and neat, but not new. It had been repaired with skill by a fine seamstress.

'I'm figuring you got yourself a job, Frances.'

She nodded. 'Yes. I'm going to Apache Springs. I'm the new station cook there. Times have been difficult lately. It was the best-paid job someone like myself could ever hope to get.'

'No kinfolk?' Dix enquired.

'Not any more, Dixie.'

Dix noticed the first man leave the outhouse and the younger passenger enter. He lifted a canteen off the side of the driver's board where it hung next to a few others. He offered it to the handsome female.

'This water was fresh drawn back at Rio Hondo,' Dix said. 'It's gotta be a lot better than the water inside that old wagon.'

She accepted it. 'Thank you.'

Dix smiled. 'We'll be in Apache Springs in about two or three hours by my reckoning. It's nice there as I recall. Has a young station manager named Rance Howard. Single fella.'

Frances blushed as she removed the stopper and raised the canteen to her lips.

'Dixie,' Dan called from beside the water wagon. Dix looked at his friend and could tell by Dan's expression that he wanted him to walk over.

Dix touched his hat brim to the drinking woman then turned and walked across the white sand to where Dan was standing. He put the Stetson over his grey hair and rested his knuckles on his gun grips.

'I'm sorry, Dan. I know ya saw her first but — '

'I ain't worried about ya talking to her.' Dan pointed off into the distance towards a wall of purple rocks and a towering mesa. 'I am kinda troubled by that, though.'

Tom Dix walked round his pal and looked out into the shimmering desert to where Dan was pointing. His eyebrows rose.

A dozen black buzzards were circling in the cloudless blue sky. Dix glanced at Dan.

'Something must be dead out there, Dan.'

'That's what I figured, Dixie,' Dan agreed. 'Something or someone.'

'Something's dead OK. There ain't

nothing else that attracts buzzards like that,' Dix said thoughtfully. 'I reckon I'll go take a look.'

Dan handed a bucket of water to his friend. 'Water your horse first, Dixie. It looks even hotter out there than it is here.'

Dix nodded as he took the bucket by its rope handle. 'Stay here until I return. Shouldn't take me long to ride out there and back.'

Dan bit his lip and tasted the dried salt that caked his face. He looked at their three passengers, then back at the man he trusted above all others.

'I'm gonna water and feed these nags slower than anyone ever done before, pard,' Dan said.

'Yeah?' Dix tightened the drawstring of his hat under his chin. 'How come?'

'I ain't going anywhere without my shotgun guard,' Dan said firmly. 'You look out for yourself, Dixie. There might just be a gun-happy varmint out there, waiting to steal himself a mount.'

Dix started towards their mounts tied

at the rear of the stagecoach. He had only taken a few steps when he tilted his head and looked back at his friend.

'Her name's Frances, Dan.' He winked. 'Miss Frances Ward.'

It was Dan's turn to blush.

10

Tom Dix stood in his stirrups as his gloved hands guided the high-shouldered horse towards the makeshift campsite set close to a wall of sun-bleached rocks. From his high vantage point he looked about the barren landscape for any hint of danger, but there was no living thing within sight. Only the black-winged buzzards, which continued to circle ominously far above him. Dix kept his horse moving towards the high mesa. Then, through the shimmering heat haze, he saw a patch of blackened ground about a hundred yards from the foot of a mountain range.

There were countless caves in the wall of rock. Most had been created by nature but a few looked as though they were the work of miners. Dix galloped his mount over a sandy crest, then his sand-filled eyes saw the bodies of the two men. He sat down and slowed his mount.

'Gold miners,' Dix muttered before correcting himself: 'Dead 'uns.'

For a brief moment Dix thought these men might have been killed for their gold dust. Then he recognized the style of senseless slaughter that confronted him. This was not the work of any sane man, he thought. This had all the hallmarks of the albino horseman he and his friends had encountered a few months earlier.

He looked harder at the dead men.

Their blood had already dried but still stained the otherwise pristine sand. Dix looked up again at the wide-winged buzzards as they floated on the warm thermals above him. They circled the two dead bodies in anticipation of the feast they would soon be enjoying. It was a chilling sight he had seen many times before. Yet it was the silence which was the most unnerving. The birds did not make a single sound.

Dix steadied his mount.

His eyes narrowed as they studied the two dead men. Both had been back-shot and worse. Dix looked at the small boulder and the two rifles still resting against it. One of the dead men had an outstretched arm. His fingers were frozen in the agony of death. They had both been trying to reach their weapons, Dix thought.

Both had failed.

Both had paid the price for trying.

Nervously, Dix swung his horse around. He tried to see if the killer had left any hint as to his identity. Then he saw the hoof tracks of their attacker's mount.

He tapped his spurs and rode to where the gunman's horse had stopped close to the remnants of the campfire. Dix then spotted the skillet and knew that both men had been attacked as they ate their supper.

He dismounted and leaned over the blackened sand.

His eyes saw the boot tracks.

Boot tracks he recognized.

Dix knelt on one knee. His eyes stared knowingly at the mark of the killer's left boot. It had a distinctive split in its leather sole, which the seasoned gunfighter had noticed a few months earlier. It was the same boot print, he told himself. His eyes darted around the area in search of the maniac who had done this but there was no one to be seen. His mind then told him that this killer only struck during the hours of darkness. He noticed the hoof tracks which had cut through the sand. They led south in the direction of Apache Springs.

He rose back up and glared through the heat haze. The rider had headed in the same direction the stagecoach was destined for. Dix took hold of the saddle horn and stepped into his stirrup.

Dix swung his right leg over the saddle and poked his right boot toe into the other stirrup as his gloved hands gathered up his long leathers. His eyes glanced down at the boot print for the last time. At last his theories were proven to be correct. The albino gunman Hickok had killed up on the high rocks months earlier had not been the Phantom at all. It had been his brother, just as he had reasoned the previous night before he and Dan had set out.

The real maniac was not dead.

After hiding out for months he had eventually crawled out from one of the caves and started his slaughtering again. Dix tried to work out why, but it was impossible for a sane mind to understand the irrational workings of a twisted brain. Then Dix felt a cold chill race up his spine in defiance of the blistering temperature of the desert.

It had all been to do with revenge three months before, Dix thought.

But the avenger had failed. Hickok was still alive and the maniac named Gunn had yet to fulfil his vow to destroy the person who had killed his father. Now there was a dead brother to avenge also.

Dix thought hard. The stagecoach driver back at Rio Hondo had not been feverish or delusional as his last words spilled from his dying lips.

He had known exactly who it was who had killed his passenger, his guard and ultimately himself. Dix felt his heart suddenly quicken. His suspicions had been proved totally correct.

'Dear God. I was right. The Phantom is alive.'

Tom Dix dragged his reins to his right and spurred. He thundered across the desert back towards the awaiting stagecoach.

There was no time to lose. Somewhere in this unholy vastness of sand the Phantom was waiting until sundown to strike. For when darkness came, so did the ruthless killer.

The sun was still high. There was plenty of time to reach Apache Springs. Dix kept telling himself that as he urged his horse on towards the waiting stagecoach.

With half-closed eyes Dix saw the

four people grow larger as he kept spurring. There was plenty of time to reach the way station and warn the people there, he thought. The sun was now at its highest and that meant they had at least six hours before sunset.

They would be safe long before darkness fell and the Phantom rode again in search of fresh prey.

Yet Dix kept frantically spurring because no matter how many times he told himself that they would reach the way station long before darkness returned to the desert, he did not believe it.

He felt as helpless as a fly who had wandered into a spider's web.

11

The light from the fiery torches flickered down from the parapet over the courtyard as Howard and Hayes carefully eased the dead body of the shotgun guard from the roof of the stage-coach. It slid on the canvas of the tailgate as the two strong men supported its lifeless weight. The driver lifted what was left of Travis Smith off the wooden protrusion and then rested the body down next to the liveryman.

'This ain't good, Rance,' the driver said as he studied the two dead men at their feet. 'Look at them. Both killed with head shots. It takes a critter with real skill to shoot someone in the head from that distance.'

Howard glanced at the driver. 'How far away was he when he made them shots, Joe?'

'Close to the crest, Rance,' Hayes

answered. 'That gotta be a quarter mile from here. Whoever he is he sure can shoot good.'

The station manager was totally stunned not just because in less than ten minutes they had been attacked by an unknown gunman twice but also by the fact that anyone could be so deadly accurate at such a distance. Howard wondered who it was and why he was aiming his wrath at them. He stared down at the bodies. He knew the two company men well but the bullets had left their dead faces unrecognizable.

Howard shuddered. Anyone who could kill from a quarter of a mile away was someone who could pick any of them off whenever he chose. All a maniac like that needed was a target and then he would kill it.

But why?

The question burned in the young station manager. There had never been any trouble at Apache Springs. Nothing that had warranted retribution as far as he could recall.

'This just don't make any sense, Joe,' Howard sighed anxiously. 'No sense at all.'

'The older ya get the more ya realize that nothing does, son.' Hayes shrugged. 'I was once married to a gal named Bessie. We had three little 'uns but none of them lived long. Then Bessie died as well. Nope, none of it makes any sense.'

Both men looked up as the door of the stagecoach was opened.

One by one the three gamblers disembarked from the stagecoach and looked at the two bodies beside the troubled driver and manager. None of them spoke as they dusted off their finery and studied their unfamiliar surroundings.

Hayes patted the station manager's arm. 'I'll bury them, Rance. I reckon ya need a stiff drink.'

Howard inhaled deeply and stopped the driver from leaving his side. 'Did ya see who it was, Joe? Did ya see who did this?'

'I thought I did but now I come to think about it I ain't so sure.' Hayes rubbed his sweat-soaked neck.

'What ya mean?'

The driver looked into the eyes of his friend. 'For just a brief moment before he opened up on us I would have sworn I caught me a glimpse of the Phantom.'

The face of Rance Howard went ashen. 'But he's dead.'

'Like I said, it was just a brief glimpse.' Hayes shrugged and started to make his way to the stables. 'I was travelling kinda fast at the time so I was probably wrong. Anyways, I'll get me a shovel. Go get that drink down ya, boy. Ya surely need it.'

'Are you the station manager?' one of the gamblers asked the befuddled Howard.

For a moment Howard did not reply. He was walking in a trance back towards the main building when the three gamblers surrounded him. The station manager paused and looked at each of them in turn.

'Reckon ya must be the gamblers,' he muttered, then continued on.

'He knows what we are,' one of them

said to the others.

'It's just a guess,' another of them said. 'It's our fancy clothes.'

The trio of passengers trailed the younger man into the the large, lamp-lit room. They all watched as Howard made his way to the bar and poured a large measure of whiskey. As they moved towards him someone spoke across the room from behind them.

'So ya finally made it.' The voice of Hickok was unmistakable.

The gamblers turned and stared at the famed gambler in shocked awe. They had all seen Hickok many times but never covered in blood before. His shirt, pants and boots were smeared in crimson gore. Blood dripped from his fingers as Hickok studied the trio of gamblers he had summoned.

Long Island Louis made his way to the lean Hickok and stopped when he saw the amount of blood coating the famed gambler.

'What happened to you, Bill?' Louis gasped. 'Are you hurt?'

'This ain't my blood, ya fool,' Hickok answered, wiping his gore-covered hands down his ruined white shirt. 'I've bin tending a wounded man back there.'

'How's Shorty, Wild Bill?' Howard walked with a glass in one hand and a bottle in the other. When he reached the long-haired Hickok he paused just long enough for the whiskey bottle to be snatched from his grip.

Hickok raised the bottle to his lips and took a long swallow of the fiery liquor. He lowered it back down and nodded to the troubled Howard.

'Relax. He ain't dead,' Hickok said. 'Reckon he'll be laid up for a week or so, though. I stitched him up after I cut out the bullet.'

The gamblers moved around Hickok like flies. They had risked their necks in order to respond to his offer of playing in the biggest poker tournament any of them had ever imagined, and were eager to start.

'What about the game, Bill?' Philo Chance asked.

'When do we start playing?' Jack West demanded.

'We rode through a war to get here, Wild Bill,' Long Island said. 'We're all itching to start playing.'

'Hold ya damn horses, boys,' Hickok scolded the three of them as his hooded eyes looked hard at the troubled manager. 'What's eating ya, boy?'

Howard shook his head. 'Luke's dead and so is the stagecoach guard.'

'Do ya figure it was the same critter that attacked the station?' Hickok queried.

'Yep.' Howard downed his glass of whiskey. 'He not only killed the guard and Luke but he killed them both with head shots from close to a quarter of a mile distance.'

'Were they lucky shots or do ya reckon he was aiming at their heads, Rance?' Hickok did not blink as he waited for the answer.

'I'm not sure anyone could get that lucky, Wild Bill.'

'Me neither.'

'When we gonna start the game, Bill?' West interrupted.

James Butler Hickok ignored the gambler and his question. All he could think about was the fact that both men had been shot in the head. It was not the type of shot most gunmen would attempt. The torso was always the easier target.

'Not many men can make that shot once, let alone twice,' he said thoughtfully. 'Only someone real confident or plumb loco would even try.'

'Joe the driver also said that he got a glimpse of the bushwhacker before he opened up on the stage, Wild Bill,' Howard told Hickok. 'He said it looked like the Phantom.'

Hickok took another swig of whiskey and sighed. His eyes burned into the gamblers like branding-irons.

'The game's delayed, boys.'

12

It was late afternoon and the mood inside the way station was getting more and more tense. The three gamblers who had travelled to Apache Springs were frustrated and had been trying to rile the famed James Butler Hickok into changing his mind and starting the poker game. Hickok downed a glass of whiskey and stared at the array of rifles spread out on the large table before him. He had greased, oiled and loaded every weapon in the way station's arsenal, yet still he did not feel any less anxious. He was surrounded by men and not one of them had any experience with guns, apart from his old poker foe Long Island Louis.

'Reckon you've loaded every damn rifle and gun in this place, Bill,' Louis remarked as he poured himself another glass of whiskey and studied it. 'Now can we play cards?'

Hickok glanced at the gambler. 'Not yet.'

West and Chance shook their heads.

'We've come a long way for this game, Bill,' Chance muttered. 'It seems to me that ya don't want to play. I sure hope ya ain't got cold feet. Are ya scared of losing?'

'That'll be the day.' Hickok pulled both his six-shooters from his holsters and spun them on his fingers. 'I can beat all three of ya.'

'Then let's ante up and start playing,' Louis said.

'We'll start when I say so.'

'Reckon we might as well head on back to Cactus Flats,' West grumbled. 'There sure ain't no action here.'

Hickok walked across the floor to where all three gamblers were seated. 'We got a couple of dead folks being buried out back and you figure there ain't no action around here?'

'I want to play poker,' Jack West snorted. 'Two dead stagecoach men ain't nothing to get excited about. We see more dead than that every Saturday night back at Cactus Flats.'

Hickok nodded. 'Sure ya do, Jack. Trouble is we're kinda trapped here by a maniac. This critter will pick us all off one by one unless we stop him. What's the point of starting the game if we have to stop halfway through?'

Louis rose and looked at Hickok. 'Are ya scared, Bill? Is the famous Wild Bill scared by some trigger-happy varmint out there?'

'I'd be real careful if I were you, Long Island,' Hickok warned angrily. 'I don't cotton to folks branding me as being yella.'

Suddenly all four men's attention was drawn to the open doorway as Howard came rushing into the large room. He removed his hat and beat it against his thigh as he closed in on the four gamblers. Hickok looked at the young man.

'Me and Joe have been checking the outside walls,' Howard said. 'Making sure that there ain't no way that damn killer can scale them when he returns.'

'You went outside?' Louis asked. 'Outside the station?'

West and Chance both stood and stared at the young station manager.

'You went out there?' West repeated the question.

'Sure.' Howard nodded. 'Everyone knows the Phantom only strikes at night.'

'Who the hell is this Phantom varmint anyway?' Louis asked. 'I've heard of most gunfighters but I ain't never heard of him.'

'Count yourself mighty lucky, Long Island,' Hickok said. He produced a cigar from his silver case and bit off its tip.

Chance moved to Louis's shoulder. Leaning over it he said:

'Night's a long way off. If this critter only strikes at night then why don't we just head out while it's still light, Long Island?'

West agreed. 'Philo's right. Let's get

out of this damn place before sundown.'

Hickok rested a hip on the edge of
the table and struck a match. He
sucked the flame into his cigar, then
blew the match out.

'How do ya all figure on travelling
from here, boys?'

Angrily Louis pointed at the door.
'There's a stagecoach out there in the
courtyard and a lot of fresh horses in
the corral just waiting to be hitched up
to the damn thing. Hell, we could be
back in Cactus Flats long before it gets
dark.'

'Now who sounds yella?' Hickok
taunted Long Island Louis through a
cloud of smoke.

'Hold on there.' Howard moved
between the two gamblers who were
eyeing one another and looked ready to
draw their guns. 'Them horses and that
stage are the property of the Overland
Stagecoach company. Nobody is taking
them anywhere. Savvy?'

'Why not?' Chance protested.

'The rules state that every stage has to have a company driver and a fully armed guard,' Howard said. 'I just buried the guard along with one of my liverymen. My other liveryman is lying back there half-dead. Ya ain't taking nothing.'

'I'm not staying here,' Jack West said. 'It's suicide.'

Hickok rose back up to his full height and smiled at his three fellow gamblers. 'Scared?'

Then the chilling sound of gunfire from somewhere outside the station's sturdy walls filled the room. Each of the men stopped in his tracks and looked at the others.

'I thought ya said the Phantom never strikes during the day?' Long Island Louis snapped at Howard. 'That sure sounds like gunfire to me.'

Hickok gripped his cigar in his teeth and dragged one of the repeating rifles off the table. 'I suggest ya all take one of these Winchesters and follow me up on to the wall, my brave boys.'

'I ain't here to do no shooting,' West argued.

'Me neither,' Chance said.

'That's up to you.' Hickok marched quickly from the room and out into the brilliant sunshine. He did not have to look behind him because he could see their shadows trailing his every step. They were all toting a rifle just as he had instructed. The ear-splitting sound of shots rang out from the desert again. This time it was from the opposite direction to the earlier attack.

'West wall.' Howard pointed.

'Ya right, Rance.' Hickok ran and mounted the steps to the parapet two at a time. 'C'mon, boys.'

13

The five men stood staring into the heat haze from the top of the high parapet above the west gate. Then the air reverberated as a rifle was fired. A moment later the thundering stagecoach came through the shimmering wall of hot vapour as Dan Shaw guided the six-horse team towards the station's gates. Seated beside him, Tom Dix held the Winchester above his head. Each of his shots was designed to alert the station that they were coming in fast.

Joe Hayes ran across the sand from the stables. The sturdy character stopped beside the secured gates and looked up at Howard.

'Who is it, Rance?' Hayes yelled.

'It's the east-bound stage,' Howard replied. He started back down the steps. 'Open them gates, Joe.'

Hickok screwed up his eyes and

stared hard at the two men sitting atop the stagecoach driver's high board. His drooping moustache hid the wry smile that etched his features as he recognized them.

'Well I'll be damned,' Hickok said. He watched the large doors being opened a few seconds before the stagecoach sped into the station courtyard. No sooner had the two horses tied to its tailgate entered the sanctuary than Hayes pushed and closed the heavy gates once more.

'What's wrong, Wild Bill?' Louis asked.

'Nothing's wrong, Long Island,' Hickok replied. He turned and started to descend the steps. 'But I'm feeling a whole lot better now than I was five minutes back.'

'How come?' Louis asked as he followed.

'Because the guard on that stagecoach just happens to be the best man with a six-shooter this side of the Pecos.' Hickok laughed as he watched Hayes securing the gates again. 'That's why, Long Island. That's why.'

The gamblers trailed Hickok across the courtyard to the stagecoach as it came to a halt outside the main station building.

Howard looked up at the two men and smiled. 'What in tarnation are you two doing on one of my stages? Did ya steal it?'

'We happen to be employees of the Overland, boy.' Dan looped the reins around the brake pole and looked down at Howard. 'The Phantom killed the crew on their way to Rio Hondo, Rance. Me and Dixie was a tad low on funds so we hired on to take this boneshaker to Cactus Flats.'

Dixie ran the tails of his bandanna over his face and dropped the rifle into the box at his feet next to the strongbox. 'We was also mighty hungry.'

Howard's expression altered as both Dan and Dix climbed down. 'Franks and Holden are dead?'

'Yep,' Dix answered. He looked at the approaching Hickok.

'And the passenger.' Dan sighed. 'We

were the only two critters hungry enough to take on the job.'

'Dixie,' Hickok called out, 'I sure am glad to see you. I see old Dan is still tagging on ya coat tails.'

'What the hell are ya doing here, James Butler?' Dix asked. He glanced at the other three gamblers behind the tall lean Hickok. 'And what are they?'

'Don't pay them no mind, Dixie.' Hickok winked. 'They're here for plucking, boy.'

'Gamblers,' Dan said knowingly. 'I thought I could smell perfume before them gates opened.'

The stagecoach door nearest to the adobe building swung open and the two male passengers disembarked. They both charged into the building. Rance Howard went to close the carriage door when the handsome female moved out into the sunlight.

Howard gasped in surprise. 'I'm sorry, ma'am. I didn't know ya was in there.'

She let his large hand take her small

one and carefully stepped down on to the sand. 'My name's Frances Ward.'

'Howdy, Miss Ward,' Howard replied with a smile that stretched from ear to ear. 'My name's Rance. I'm the station manager.'

'And I'm your new cook,' she said in a low, sultry voice.

'Ya are? Things are sure looking up.' Howard grinned and watched her enter the main building.

Dan shrugged. 'I sure hope she can cook.'

Howard glanced at Dan. 'Who cares? Anyone that looks that good can burn water for all I care.'

'Damn!' Dan shook his head and watched the smiling station manager trail the handsome female into the building.

Hickok wrapped his arms around his old friend's shoulders and leaned down so that his words would only be heard by him. 'Ya right about the Phantom. He's on the loose again, boys. He attacked here twice last night and killed a couple of the stagecoach boys before he rode out.'

'He also killed two miners out in the desert,' Dix said. 'I found their bodies.'

Thoughtfully Hickok straightened up to his full height and looked at the sky. The sun was low and the shadows were dark and long. 'How many times have I gotta kill that bastard, boys?'

'He sure don't die easy, James Butler.' Dix nodded.

14

Not willing to wait for darkness and the inevitable return of the murderous Phantom to strike at the way station again, the intrepid trio of Hickok, Dix and Shaw had decided to follow the hoof tracks left by their mortal enemy back to his lair. Hickok knew only too well that the only way to defeat an enemy as dangerous as the Phantom was to strike first. He had defeated two of the Gunn menfolk that way and had no intention of treating the last of them any differently.

All he and his pals had to do was reach Gunn before Gunn reached them. It sounded simple enough, but all three of the riders knew the truth. Facing gunfighters was never easy and when those gunfighters were also lunatics it tended to become almost suicidal.

Killing people had never been something Hickok had really savoured but
there were times when a man had to act
first if he were to stop further atrocities.
This was one of those times.

Although the sun was low even
before they had set out from the way
station each of them knew they had
enough time to reach the mountains
before it set. At least, they hoped they
had enough time.

James Butler Hickok sat astride his
elegant appaloosa mare and led Dix
and Dan across the white sand towards
the mountain range and the high mesas
like a general leading his troops into
battle.

The tracks left by the Phantom's grey
stallion were still clear in the otherwise
undisturbed sand. The experienced
ex-army scout knew that as long as he
kept following them they would eventually lead him and his companions to the
Phantom. The three horsemen realized
that to find Gunn after sunset would
prove to be a whole lot different from

discovering him during daylight. Enio Gunn existed only during the hours of darkness.

He was like a bat on the wing when stars filled the sky. A vicious foe, whom it was hard to better. Daylight was when the albino slayer was at his most vulnerable.

They had to reach him before sundown.

Yet the shadows had stretched like black fingers across the desert sand and were growing with every beat of their horses' hoofs.

Night was coming fast. Time was running out like sand through an upturned hourglass.

Dan spurred and drew level with his two pals.

'How long do ya figure we got until sundown?' Dan shouted.

Hickok did not answer. His hooded, unblinking eyes were fixed on the rocky barrier ahead of them like an eagle seeking its prey. The rocky lower slopes of the mountain were honeycombed with caves, in any one of which the Phantom could be hiding as he waited patiently for nightfall.

Dan moved his horse closer to Dix. 'How much time we got, Dixie? I sure don't like the idea of us tackling that maniac again after sundown.'

Dix tilted his head and looked at his friend. 'We got maybe an hour of daylight left, if we're lucky.'

'What if we ain't lucky?'

'I'd not like to try and figure that out until it happens, Dan,' Dix answered. He looked at the impressive figure of Hickok, who was spurring his horse to find even greater pace. 'I figure James Butler reckons we can get there before sundown. Leastways I sure hope he does.'

'Gunn ain't the kind of varmint who'll take kindly to our invading his hideout,' Dan said. 'I still recall the last fight we had with him.'

Dix nodded. 'We were fighting two of the Gunn boys that night, Dan. We just didn't know it.'

'They sure looked alike,' Dan recalled with a shudder. 'I never dreamed we were fighting two of them.'

'This time we're only gonna be fighting one man.' Dix grinned. 'Three against one are mighty good odds.'

The three riders spurred harder. They were closing in on the rocks quickly but the black shadows were growing and spreading across the desert even faster. Clouds of dust rose up from their horses' hoofs and hung in the still air. Mile after mile they forged on. The mountains grew larger the closer they got to them. With each stride of the appaloosa Hickok continued to study the deep tracks of the man they hunted.

Then, apparently for no reason that his companions could understand, Hickok drew rein and stopped his mount. Dust flew up and continued to float off towards the rocks as Dix and Dan halted their horses beside the appaloosa. Hickok remained expressionless as his hooded eyes surveyed the mountains and their numerous caves.

'Why'd ya stop, Wild Bill?' Dan asked, steadying his horse next to the high-shouldered mare.

Dix looked at Dan. 'James Butler must have his reasons, pard. He never does anything without good reason.'

Hickok gave a brief glance at Dix, the man who had saved his bacon on more than one occasion.

'I always said ya was mighty smart, Dixie,' Hickok said. He leaned back and slid his hand into one of the satchels of his saddle-bags.

Both men watched as Hickok withdrew a pair of binoculars and raised them to his eyes. He adjusted its focus wheel and then gave out a satisfied sigh.

'Now that sure is mighty interesting,' Hickok said.

'Can ya see him?' Dan squinted hard at the mountains, which were darkening as the sun sank lower in the heavens.

'What can ya see, James Butler?' Dix asked.

Hickok handed the field glasses to his

friend and pointed a gloved finger. 'Take a look, Dixie. Just to the left of that gully.'

Dix did as he was told. He focused the binoculars and then saw the flickering of a fire in the mouth of one of the caves. He could see movement within the cave's blackness. A shadow danced on the cave walls. Someone was moving up there, Dix thought.

'I see him.'

'Do ya?' Hickok placed a cigar between his teeth and bit off its tip. He spat at the sand and then scratched a match across his silver saddle horn. He cupped the flame and sucked in smoke as his eyes remained fixed on the distant cave and its betraying fire.

'What ya mean?' Dix lowered the binoculars. 'I can see someone moving up there in that cave. Are ya telling me it ain't the Phantom?'

Hickok nodded his head slowly. 'Do ya happen to recall me telling ya about Axil Gunn having himself two sons, Dixie?'

'Sure I do.'

A long line of smoke drifted from Hickok's mouth. 'What else did I tell ya?'

'He had himself a Cree woman,' Dan said.

'Right.' Hickok inhaled more smoke thoughtfully. 'Where did she go? We trailed the Phantom to those caves down yonder a few months back and his brother was there. We killed the wrong brother, but think about it, boys. Do ya reckon Gunn's brother was there on his lonesome? What if she's still alive? What if she's still looking after her last surviving son?'

Confused, Dix handed the binoculars back and watched as Hickok returned them to his bags. 'Are ya telling us that the Cree woman is up there?'

'What if she is, Bill?' Dan wondered.

Hickok looked at the sky again. 'I'm just telling ya that we might still have us two enemies to handle. We made the mistake before of thinking there was only one Phantom. That nearly cost us dearly. A mother can be a mighty vicious critter when her offspring are in danger. All I'm saying is that if she's still alive and up there with Gunn, we'd best be mindful of that.'

Both Dan and Dix nodded in agreement.

'Reckon ya right, James Butler.' Dix gathered in his long leathers.

'We'd best watch our backs when we do manage to get up there.' Hickok was about to spur his appaloosa into action once again when there came a flash in the mouth of the cave. Then a noise like distant thunder filled their ears. A telltale cloud of smoke came from the cave. Hickok held his horse in check as another noise came to their ears. This time it was a sickening sound.

Dan's horse gave out a dying whinny as its head was knocked backwards by the impact of a rifle bullet. A plume of blood sprayed up into the fading rays of the sun. The horse bucked as all horses buck when death unexpectedly greets them. The pitiful creature stumbled and fell, sending its stunned master somer-saulting across the sand.

Defiantly Hickok reached down, drew his Winchester from its scabbard and cocked its mechanism. He swiftly raised the rifle to his shoulder and returned fire. Then he primed the weapon again.

'Are ya OK, Dan?' Hickok snarled through cigar smoke. He squeezed his trigger again, sending another red-hot taper of lead up towards their unseen attacker.

'He's just shook up,' Dix shouted, then he fired one of his Colts across the desert towards the cave.

'What happened?' Dan staggered to his feet as Dix moved his mount close to the shaken old lawman. Dix reached out with his left arm and pulled his boot from its stirrup.

'Get up behind me, pard,' Dix said as another bullet came cutting through the dry desert air from the far-off cave.

Dan took his pal's arm, poked a boot in the vacant stirrup and managed to climb up behind Dix. He sat on the bedroll behind the saddle cantle and wrapped his arms around his friend's waist.

Dix swung his mount around. 'I got him.'

Hickok cocked and fired his rifle three more times. Then he glanced over his shoulder at the two men atop Dix's horse.

'C'mon, boys. We gotta reach them shadows mighty fast. We're sitting ducks out here.'

The two horses thundered towards the foot of the high mountains and the black shadows that stretched away from them. Now each man silently prayed that darkness would come quickly, for they knew that it might prove to be their only protection.

15

Hickok reached the foot of the steep, rocky slope first and leapt from his appaloosa just as Dix reined in beside him. The last rays of the sun had faded off in the distance and the desert was plunged into an eerie hue that only starlight could create. The shadows were black in the narrow gully they found themselves in. They had ridden through a storm of bullets, which had only ended when the Phantom's rifle had run out of ammunition and needed to be reloaded. The three men managed to find enough brush to secure their reins, then they looked up at the strange array of rocks that towered over them.

'How in tarnation are we gonna get up there?' Dan asked. He leaned against the rocks and checked his six-shooter. 'I ain't no mountain goat even if I looks like one.'

Dix studied the slope of rock. 'There has to be another way up there.'

'Ya right, Dixie.' Hickok looked all around them as he tried to work out how their deadly enemy had managed to reach the cave from where he had opened fire. 'There has to be another way to reach those caves. All we gotta do is find it.'

'Or find his horse,' Dan said.

Dix and Hickok both looked at their pal. Dan felt uneasy.

'Dan's right. There ain't no way that critter could take a horse up there. The animal has to be down here someplace,' Dix said.

Hickok nodded and pulled the cigar from his lips. 'Hold on a minute.'

Dan and Dix moved closer to Hickok as the tall man knelt and studied the sand at their feet. Even the starlight could not conceal the hoof tracks from the old scout's hooded glare.

'What ya see, Bill?' Dan asked.

Dix pointed at the ground. 'Hoof tracks. Even I can see them.'

Hickok tilted his head. 'Not just hoof tracks, Dixie. I see me wheel tracks as well.'

'Wheel tracks?' Dan gasped. 'Ya mean he got himself a wagon as well as a horse?'

'Yep.' Hickok returned to his full height, sucked the last of the smoke from his cigar, then tossed it aside. 'A wagon pulled by an ox. A real powerful ox.'

'What the hell would he want that for?' Dix wondered.

'Let's go find out.' Hickok indicated for them to follow him as he walked along the gully, trailing the vehicle that had left its betraying marks in the sand. As they reached the very end of the gully the three men saw the covered wagon, the ox and the grey stallion. Hickok did not stop walking until he reached the wagon's front wheel.

Hickok screwed up his eyes and studied the churned-up sand carefully. Then he looked at his companions.

'The Cree woman was driving the

wagon,' Hickok explained knowingly. He pointed to the blackest section of the gully. 'Her footprints head off thataway.'

'That must be the way up to the caves,' Dix reasoned.

'Yep,' Hickok agreed.

'Do we follow or do we stay here and wait, James Butler?' Dix asked.

Dan looked edgy. 'I don't like to mention it but it's dark, boys. We'd better be ready to bump into the Phantom any time soon.'

'He knows we're down here,' Hickok said coldly as he drew one of his guns and cocked its trigger. 'He saw us riding right to the foot of the mountain. He's gotta figure that we'll be waiting for him to show himself.'

'He can't just stay up in the caves, though,' Dix ventured. 'Even a loco-bean knows that come sunrise we'll be going up there after him. He don't like the sun. If he's gonna try and kill us he has to do it now.'

The words had only just left the lips

of the veteran gunfighter when the three men heard the sound of boots on rock above them. They turned and saw the awesome sight of the albino slaughterer with a rifle cradled in his hands, bathed in the eerie light of a myriad stars.

'The Phantom,' Dan gasped.

'That's right,' Gunn screamed down at them. 'The Phantom can't be killed but you can, Hickok. Ya gonna pay for what ya done to my pa and brother. Pay with ya life.'

The three men saw the rifle's metal barrel glint as Gunn turned it on them.

'Take cover!' Hickok shouted. He turned faster than the blink of an eye and raised his Colt. The palm of his left hand fanned the gun hammer. Deafening shots and blinding flashes of lead spewed upward as Gunn squeezed the trigger of his rifle.

Hickok's tall, lean frame was punched off his feet as the rifle bullet tore through the sleeve of his buckskin jacket. As he hit the wall of rock Dix leapt forward and drew both his guns. He fired a half-dozen shells from his matched .45s up at the ledge but no sooner had the gunsmoke left his Winchester's barrel than the Phantom had vanished.

Hickok slid on to the ground and angrily stared through glazed eyes at the blood that seeped from the hole in his left jacket sleeve. 'Damn it all. This jacket was given to me by George Custer.'

Dan fired his gun blindly up at the rocks, then knelt beside the wounded Hickok.

'I never knew ya was sentimental, Wild Bill,' Dan said. Then he saw Dix running towards the darkest part of the gully.

'Sentiment ain't got nothing to do with it, Dan,' Hickok growled. 'Do ya know how much this jacket is worth? It's worth more than my horse.'

Dix ran into the shadows and then heard the distinctive sound of a gun being cocked somewhere to his right. He turned on his heel just as a bright flash and an ear-splitting shot exploded around him. Dix felt the heat of the bullet as it passed close to his face.

Instinctively Dix fired both his six-shooters. He heard a groan, then a body hit the ground.

'Got him!' Dix whispered to himself. He cautiously cocked the hammers of both his weapons again and crept deeper into the blackness. His boot toe touched something. Dix stopped, holstered one of his smoking guns, crouched and reached down. His hand touched the body. He rose back up and turned to look over his shoulder. He could just make out the shapes of Dan and Hickok close to where the famed gunfighter had been felled by the rifle shot.

'I reckon I got him, boys,' Dix shouted out.

Hickok managed to get to his feet. Then, using Dan as a human crutch, he made his way beside the retired lawman into the darkness.

'Ya sure, Dixie?' Dan asked his partner. 'Ya sure ya killed him?'

'Well, there's something dead by my boots,' Dix answered.

'Let's take a look.' Hickok pulled out a match from his jacket pocket and struck it against a flat piece of rock. The flame illuminated the body. All three men stared down at the old Cree woman's corpse. 'Damn it all! Gunn's still alive up there someplace.'

Dix looked ahead of them just before the match's flame went out. What he had briefly seen was like a natural staircase created by aeons of natural erosion. 'Reckon that's the way up to the caves, boys.'

Dan shook his head. 'We can't head on up there without ending up as dead as this old woman. Gunn ain't gonna be taking no prisoners when he realizes his mother is dead, Dixie.'

'Dan's right, Dixie.' Hickok rammed his gun into its holster and gripped his arm. Blood trickled through his fingers. 'We gotta try and lure him down or make him show himself.'

Dix brooded. He knew they were

right but every sinew in his body wanted to find the deadly Phantom and end his tyranny once and for all. 'What do ya suggest we do to draw him out again, James Butler?'

'Hold on a minute, Dixie.' Hickok reached down to his gunbelt and pulled his knife from it. He handed it to Dan. 'Cut off a couple of the leather fringes from my jacket and tie them around my arm, Dan. I'm bleeding like a pig.'

Dan did as he was asked and stemmed the flow of blood from the bullet hole with the crude but effective tourniquet. As his partner worked on Hickok, Dix moved away from the two men and listened to the movement above them. Boot leather on rock had a sound all of its own.

'He's moving back to where his horse and the wagon are, boys,' Dix whispered. 'If he climbs down he'll be able to kill our horses and ride that grey stallion of his away from here.'

Dan looked troubled. 'I don't reckon we'll last long out here in the desert without our horses.'

'Me neither,' Hickok agreed. He defied his pain and strode back out into the starlight. 'C'mon. I got me an idea.'

They hurried back to where the wagon stood. With each step they kept looking up at the rocks. Each knew Gunn could reappear at any moment and start shooting again.

They reached the covered wagon and Hickok looked over its tailgate into the dark interior. There were sacks of flour and a bale of hay for the animals stacked in there.

Hickok turned to both his friends. 'Keep ya weapons trained up there. I got me a feeling the Phantom's gonna show himself real soon.'

Dix cocked both his six-shooters as Dan held his own .45 at arm's length. Both men aimed up at the ledge as Hickok produced another match and struck it against the tailgate of the stationary wagon. He raised the flame and held it at the canvas until it caught fire. Then Hickok dropped the match on to the nearest of the sacks.

Within seconds the wagon was ablaze.

Flames swept across the kindling-dry bed of the vehicle as its canopy was engulfed by fire. The gully was lit up like a Fourth of July bonfire.

Suddenly Gunn appeared, like the mythical creature he called himself. The maniac started frantically to shoot his rifle down into the gully as Dan and Dix returned fire. Bullets criss-crossed between the ridge and the floor of the gully as the men tried feverishly to destroy one another.

The wounded Hickok slowly drew one of his guns, cocked its hammer and took aim. As choking gunsmoke filled the air the tall man with the mane of long dark hair trained his gun sight on Enio Gunn.

Hickok squeezed the trigger once. His shot was lethal. As his hooded eyes stared upward he lowered the weapon. The Phantom buckled, then moved unsteadily forward towards the rim of the ledge. The rifle fell from his hands.

With blood pouring from the hole in the centre of his shirt front the Phantom toppled over the ledge. He fell from the high rocks through the smoke-filled air and landed on the blazing bed of the burning covered wagon. Millions of sparks rose into the air.

Within seconds the smell of burning flesh filled the gully as the last of the Gunn clan was turned into blackened ash.

Dix moved to Hickok. 'C'mon. Ya finished it, James Butler. Ya killed the Phantom.'

Hickok watched the fiery wagon and the charred remains at its centre. He made no attempt to move.

'Are ya coming, Bill?' Dan asked his wounded pal. 'Let's get back to Apache Springs so we can tend to that wound of yours properly.'

'I ain't going anywhere until the fire's out, boys,' Hickok told them. 'I'm gonna make sure he's really dead this time. I'm tired of killing the same critter over and over again.'

Finale

The heart of the way station was warming as the rays of a new day filled the interior of the large room. Tom Dix and Dan Shaw sat beside the bar and shared a bottle of whiskey as they watched the last throes of the long poker game. The three gamblers sat across the table from Hickok and watched as the man with an arm in a sling stared at the five cards in his hand. The pot was the biggest any of them had ever played for and each man had held out until his very last poker chip had been pushed into the centre of the table.

Jack West and Philo Chance had already folded and were watching as Long Island Louis chewed on his cigar with his own five cards in his hand. Both men wondered if Louis had the hand which would ultimately defeat Hickok.

'Are ya getting nervous, Wild Bill?' Louis asked.

'That'll be the day, Long Island,' Hickok replied through a cloud of cigar smoke.

Dix and Dan inhaled the aroma of the meal that was being prepared by the station's attractive new cook. They said nothing as Rance Howard walked across the large room with his hair freshly oiled and combed. They looked at one another and gave a knowing nod as the young station manager continued on into the kitchen.

'I got me feeling that Rance has been roped and branded by that pretty lady, Dix.' Dan grinned.

Dix nodded. 'I reckon ya right, Dan.'

The gamblers continued to taunt one another as each of them delayed showing his hand.

'James Butler sure recovered fast, Dan,' Dix said. He filled their glasses with whiskey again. 'Ya only cut the lead out of his arm three hours back by my reckoning.'

'And he was at the table less than an hour after I sewed him up.' Dan lifted the glass and took a sip. 'Ya figure he's gonna win?'

Dixie smiled. 'Sure he will. He's got vinegar.'

Dan leaned close to his pal and whispered:

'He's also got four aces hidden in the sling, Dixie.'

We do hope that you have enjoyed reading this large print book.

Did you know that all of our titles are available for purchase?

We publish a wide range of high quality large print books including:
Romances, Mysteries, Classics General Fiction Non Fiction and Westerns

Special interest titles available in large print are:
The Little Oxford Dictionary Music Book, Song Book Hymn Book, Service Book

Also available from us courtesy of Oxford University Press:
Young Readers' Dictionary (large print edition) Young Readers' Thesaurus (large print edition)

For further information or a free brochure, please contact us at:
**Ulverscroft Large Print Books Ltd., The Green, Bradgate Road, Anstey, Leicester, LE7 7FU, England.
Tel:** (00 44) 0116 236 4325
Fax: (00 44) 0116 234 0205

DALTON AND THE SUNDOWN KID

Ed Law

When Dalton rides into Lonetree looking for work, he finds a town crippled by the local outlaw — the Sundown Kid. Tasked with resolving the Kid's latest kidnapping, Dalton must deliver a ransom to the bandit to secure the safe return of young Sera. Culver. However, before he reaches the rendezvous point, the ransom is stolen. Then a fearsome shootout leaves him stranded in the wilderness . . . With the fate of a woman at stake, can Dalton fight the good fight and prevail?

THE AFTERLIFE OF SLIM McCORD

Jack Martin

Rogues Blackman and Tanner have seen it all, but nothing has prepared them for what they find in the town of Possum Creek: the preserved corpse of their long-ago compadre, the outlaw Slim McCord, being exhibited in a travelling carny show! Outraged, the pair decide to steal him away and give his mortal remains a decent burial. But before he is laid to rest, Slim will take part in one last bank job alongside his old friends . . .

COMANCHE MOON

Simon Webb

The Reverend Jonas Faulkner, pastor of the First Claremont Presbyterian Church in Texas, is a man with a secret: in his younger days he was a notorious gunman, involved in a crime which resulted in the deaths of several children. So when six young girls, travelling to an orphanage in Calermont, are seized by a Kiowa raiding party, Pastor Faulkner knows he must act in atonement for his past sins. For the elderly clergyman is still a force to be reckoned with . . .

THE HOT SPURS

Boyd Cassidy

When the riders of the Bar 10 run up against an escaped prisoner and his ruthless gang, they find themselves in deep trouble. Bret Jarvis and his henchmen are heading to Mexico, where men of the Circle J ranch have returned from a profitable cattle drive — making them sitting targets for a raid. But Gene Adams and his Bar 10 cowboys are soon in hot pursuit — all they need to do is stop the outlaws before they reach the border . . .

LONG RIDIN' MAN

Jake Douglas

They call him 'Hunter'. There is one man in particular for whom he searches: the man who destroyed his family. Trailing the killer, Hunter finds himself in a booming town short of one deputy sheriff: in need of cash, he pins on the badge. But the folk of Cimarron begin to wonder just who they've hired as their peacemaker. Once Hunter discovers why the town needed a fast gun so urgently, the odds are that it will be too late for him to get out alive . . .